"Shannon, sometimes one primitive emotion —like fear—will trigger another one," Derek said huskily. "It's natural."

"Is it?" She was staring up at him, her voice slow and wondering, dazed. She felt as if she'd fallen over the brink of something, was still falling wildly, and couldn't do a thing to save herself. "I've never felt this way before."

He knew what he should have done. He should have pulled her arms from around his waist, changed the subject, something. That was what he should have done.

But he had to kiss her, the way a starving man needs sustenance. His need for her was as primitive as the need for the security she'd felt when she'd leapt into his arms at the car's backfire.

At the first touch of her cool, trembling lips, what should have been a tentative first kiss exploded between them violently. Shannon, stiffened, almost crying out, and then her arms tightened fiercely around his waist as she melted against him. Everything inside her detonated, leaving behind nothing but a searing need. . . .

WHAT ARE *LOVESWEPT* ROMANCES?

They are stories of true romance and touching emotion. We believe those two very important ingredients are constants in our highly sensual and very believable stories in the *LOVESWEPT* line. Our goal is to give you, the reader, stories of consistently high quality that may sometimes make you laugh, sometimes make you cry, but are always fresh and creative and contain many delightful surprises within their pages.

Most romance fans read an enormous number of books. Those they truly love, they keep. Others may be traded with friends and soon forgotten. We hope that each *LOVESWEPT* romance will be a treasure—a "keeper." We will always try to publish

LOVE STORIES YOU'LL NEVER FORGET
BY AUTHORS YOU'LL ALWAYS REMEMBER

The Editors

LOVESWEPT® • 256

Kay Hooper
Outlaw Derek

BANTAM BOOKS
TORONTO • NEW YORK • LONDON • SYDNEY • AUCKLAND

OUTLAW DEREK

A Bantam Book / May 1988

LOVESWEPT® and the wave device are registered
trademarks of Bantam Books. Registered in U.S. Patent
and Trademark Office and elsewhere.

If you would be interested in receiving protective vinyl
covers for your Loveswept books, please write to this address
for information:

Loveswept
Bantam Books
P.O. Box 985
Hicksville, NY 11802

ISBN 0-553-21895-6

Published simultaneously in the United States and Canada

Bantam Books are published by Bantam Books, a division
of Bantam Doubleday Dell Publishing Group, Inc. Its trademark, consisting of the words "Bantam Books" and the
portrayal of a rooster, is Registered in U.S. Patent and
Trademark Office and in other countries. Marca Registrada.
Bantam Books, 666 Fifth Avenue, New York, New York 10103.

One

Derek Ross struggled up through the heavy layers of jet-lag exhaustion with an awful buzzing in his ears. Rolling over in a tangle of bedclothes, he started to reach for the phone on the nightstand, but then recognized the sound he heard. Sitting up instead, he raked his fingers through his hair.

The door. In the middle of the night. No. He looked blearily at the clock on his nightstand. At four A.M. A visitor? Even in exhaustion, his mind automatically considered and rejected possibilities of felonious intent. It wasn't likely. In general, the guys in the black hats didn't lean on door buzzers to announce their arrival, especially at four in the morning, when stealth tended to be a prime consideration.

He kicked the blankets away and got up, finding his jeans in the darkness and struggling into them to the accompaniment of a few sleepy curses. He turned on lights as he made his way through the apartment to the front door, and, when he reached it, said in a voice little more than a growl, "Yeah, what?"

"Mr. Ross? I need to talk to you."

Standing well to one side of the still-closed door, Derek frowned. A woman whose voice he didn't recognize. In his business, that tended to be a bad sign. He realized that he had tensed. "It's four o'clock in the morning," he said shortly. "Who are you, and what do you want?"

"Mr. Ross, please, I—I have to see you. It's very important."

Derek hesitated, then leaned forward cautiously so that he could look through the security peephole. He was taking a chance, because the door was composed of only a few flimsy layers of plywood, which wouldn't stop a bullet or withstand even a well-placed kick. His view through the tiny hole was distorted, but he saw enough to make him relax—if only a bit. "Hold your hands where I can see them," he said curtly.

Outside in the well-lighted hallway, the woman held both hands up at shoulder height, palms out toward him. She didn't seem surprised by his extreme caution, but then, she was obviously too distraught to be surprised by anything.

"Keep them up," he said, and drew back away from the door as he unlocked and opened it. Instantly, the woman came into the apartment, her helds still held at shoulder height. Derek closed and relocked the door.

"I'm not armed," she said softly.

He was reasonably sure of that; it was why he had relaxed. The silk dress she wore clung like a second skin and left little to the imagination. She couldn't have hidden a bullet under the garment, much less a gun. But he hadn't lived to be thirty-five by being reckless or taking unnecessary chances, so he kept his distance while watching her intently. "All right. Into the den, straight ahead."

Following her, Derek observed thoughtfully that her walk didn't fit the dress. She had the carriage of an athlete or dancer, fluid and graceful in spite of an obvious limp. The dress, on the other hand, was designed to emphasize curves and wiggles, in fact to make it nearly impossible for a woman to walk in it *without* wiggling. She managed, however, despite the limp; the slight sway of her hips was utterly feminine, but in no way exaggerated.

Still seductive as hell, though.

She stopped by the couch, continuing to hold her hands as he'd instructed. "Can—can I sit down?"

Derek circled slowly until they faced each other. "I don't know," he said dryly. "Can you?"

She blinked, then glanced down at the bright red, skintight sheath. A flush lightly colored her pale face. "Oh. I haven't sat down since—Well."

"Try," he invited her.

She did, gingerly. And managed the feat, although the strapless bodice might have slipped downward half an inch or so. An unconscious relief filled her expression as the weight was removed from her legs. Slowly, she lowered her hands until they twined together in her lap.

For a long moment, they studied each other in silence. She saw a big man, barefooted and beard-stubbled, his wheat-gold hair tousled and a thick mat of golden hair covering his powerful chest. He had very dark and lazy eyes and a way of standing that was seemingly relaxed and negligent, but gave an impression of latent strength casually under control. And he had a face that would fascinate women and artists, because it was starkly male, diamond-hard, and utterly beautiful, even though he was obviously very tired.

He saw a young woman somewhere in her twenties, of medium height and slender in a way most women wanted to be and few were: she was full-breasted, her hips curved gently, and there wasn't an ounce of excess flesh anywhere. Her hair was a rich dark brown with red highlights, falling past her shoulders in a thick mass of loose curls. Her face was heart-shaped and delicate, and she had large eyes so light brown they were almost amber, eyes with haunting shadows of pain. She looked lovely, fragile, gentle . . . and scared. Scared to death.

"Who are you?" he asked abruptly.

"Shannon." Her gaze flickered. "Brown."

"Well, it's better than 'Smith,' I suppose."

"It's my name, Mr. Ross."

He let it go. "And how do you happen to know mine?"

"I—someone gave me your name."

"Who?"

She worried her lower lip with small white teeth for a long moment. "I was told not to mention his name if I could help it."

"There's the door," Derek told her politely.

Her eyes seemed to grow larger. "He said you were hard," she murmured. "Tough without hav-

ing to act like it. But he said you'd help me if I
ever needed help. I need help."

"Who?" Derek repeated.

She sighed. "William Franklin."

"*Governor* Franklin?"

"Yes. He—over a year ago, he gave me your name.
He said you could be trusted, no matter what the
problem. And he said you were very good at what
you do."

"Did he happen to mention what I do?" Derek
asked, no expression at all in his deep voice.

Her eyes flickered, then steadied on his face.
"He said you were sort of a troubleshooter. For
different government agencies sometimes and free-
lance sometimes. He said that you take care of
problems, any kind of problems. He said . . ."

"What?" Derek asked when her voice trailed into
silence.

Very softly, she said, "He told me you could be
a—a bastard when you wanted to, but you were
honest. And that you weren't afraid of anything."

Derek shook his head. "That sounds like him."
He remembered several years back when a blackmail threat had almost cost Franklin his political
career. Looking intently at Shannon "Brown," he
said slowly. "The governor's happily married, or
was the last time I saw him. What are you to
him?"

"He's a friend."

"Uh-huh."

Her chin lifted and the big eyes flashed gold.
"He was right," she said in a shaking voice. "You
can be a bastard!"

Very dryly, Derek said, "Look, Miss *Brown*, mine
isn't a name that people like governors hand out

to casual acquaintances. If Franklin gave you my name a year ago, it was either because you and he are very, very close, or else because he knew you were in some kind of trouble, or likely to be, and it was the kind that required my brand of problem solving. Which is it?"

She bit her lip. "All right, then. We are close, but not the way you obviously think. He's my uncle."

Derek sat down in a chair, relaxing in a boneless manner that was totally deceptive. "Blood uncle?" His face indicated nothing, neither belief nor disbelief.

"Yes."

"You just wrote a new chapter in science."

She blinked. "What—what do you mean?"

"Franklin's an only child. So's his wife. Try again."

Shannon slumped, and her lips twisted in a painful little grimace. "I don't want to lie! But you won't believe it was innocent—"

"Try me."

After a moment, she nodded. "All right. I worked on his campaign, that's how we met. I was just another campaign worker at first. But then I—I got hurt. Anyway, he's a kind man, and he felt sorry for me. After the campaign, he got me a job with Civatech. Do you—?"

"I know of Civatech. High-security firm. They have an in-house think tank and an unsurpassed record at designing and manufacturing electronic toys for the military to play with. And your job?"

"Secretary, receptionist. I have a low-level security clearance: I don't work with highly classified information. I just type correspondence, answer the phone. That sort of thing."

Derek was frowning. "So you've been with Civatech about eighteen months?" He waited for her nod. "I gather Governor Franklin keeps in touch with you?"

She nodded again. "A call now and then. And he invites me to private parties he and Annie have."

"Does he ask about your work?"

Her chin lifted. "He didn't put me at Civatech to spy for him, if that's what you're implying. There's no reason he should have; Civatech usually contracts with the military, not state government. William wouldn't—"

"I didn't say he would," Derek Ross interrupted mildly. "In fact, I'm reasonably sure he wouldn't. I'm just trying to put this together. Why did he give you my name?"

She hesitated, staring at him, then appeared to make up her mind. "About a year ago, while I was having dinner with William and Annie, I mentioned that some of the letters I'd been typing seemed odd. I'm a good typist, and I read what I type instead of just scanning the words. If you know what I mean?"

"Yes."

"Two or three of the letters bothered me, because they didn't seem to make sense to me. It was nothing definite, just a sentence here and there that seemed out of place. I mentioned it to William."

"What was his reaction?"

It was impossible to tell whether Derek believed her or not, but she didn't let doubt throw her off balance. "He seemed a little puzzled at first. Then he was more bothered by it. A couple of weeks later, he asked me if there had been any more letters like that. I said no. That was when he told me about you. He made it—conversational. We were alone in the room, and he was offhand about it, even laughing. He said you'd helped him out of some trouble once, and that you were very good at what you did. He said if I was ever in trouble, I should tell you all about it."

"It didn't surprise you that he should talk that way?"

"Yes. Oh, yes. But he was so casual! And I could tell he didn't want me to ask questions, so I didn't." She hesitated, then added, "Several times these last months if no one could overhear, he'd ask kind of teasingly if I remembered who to go to if I needed help. I'd say your name, and he'd say, 'Don't forget it.' So I didn't forget."

After a moment, Derek rose abruptly and left the room. He returned seconds later with a light blanket, which he dropped around Shannon's bare shoulders. "You look frozen," he said somewhat gruffly. "Coffee?"

"Please," she said gratefully, drawing the blanket around her. She got up and followed him into the kitchen, beginning to feel less cold in more ways than physically. There was something comforting, she thought, in the mere presence of this man. He was hard and blunt and suspicious, but there was something infinitely understanding in his eyes, tolerant, as if nothing she or anyone could ever say would surprise him, and she felt safe for the first time in hours.

He didn't seem to find it surprising that she

followed him, merely gesturing for her to sit on one of the low stools at the breakfast bar. "How did you find my apartment—the phone directory?"

"Yes. William said you kept a listed phone number, even though you shouldn't."

Derek got the coffee started, then leaned back against the counter and studied her silently and quite openly. There was a package of cigarettes and a lighter on the counter, and he reached for them without looking, lighting a cigarette while continuing to look intently at her.

"You . . . you do believe me?" she asked.

Without answering that, he said, "No purse, no coat or wrap of any kind. A dress that would get you arrested if you stood on the right corner—and especially if you stood on the wrong one. And you've done a hell of a lot of walking in shoes not designed for that. So tell me what happened in the last ten hours or so that brought you to my door at four A.M."

Shannon hugged the blanket tighter around her body and took a deep breath. "Today—yesterday— just before five, I took one of those odd letters to my supervisor. It was odd in a different way from the others; it was referring to a design that was scrapped months ago, and discussed the shipment of the finished product, which was a prototype, to a foreign company I couldn't find listed in our computer, or in the city where it was supposedly based."

"Two suspicious items," Derek mused. "A supposedly nonexistent product shipped to a nonexistent company. What did your supervisor say about it?"

"That he'd look into it. He seemed impatient

and I was afraid he'd dismiss it without checking, so I mentioned the other odd letters."

Derek half closed his eyes and nodded. "Uh-huh. So you very honestly told him about things you should never have noticed. And I suppose all these odd letters came from the same source?"

Shannon nodded. "From Civatech's director of design, Adam Moreton."

"Do you always take care of his correspondence?"

"No. Only when his private secretary is sick."

He nodded. "Okay. So what happened then?"

"I went home to my apartment." Her face went completely white then, and her eyes looked enormous. "There was a party I was supposed to go to, and I went by a friend's house first to change into this dress; it's hers and she wanted me to wear it. I walked to my apartment from her place to finish getting ready, and unlocked the door. I had just pushed it open when my landlady called me from the first floor to tell me she'd signed for a package. I went to get the package. It was from my mother," she added inconsequentially.

After a moment, Derek said quietly, "What happened after you went downstairs?"

She looked at him blindly. "The explosion . . . knocked me down as I was coming back up the stairs . . . everything was bright . . . when I got up . . . and hot . . . and the apartment—my apartment—was just gone. . . ."

Derek turned to jab his cigarette into an ashtray on the counter before reaching into a cabinet and pulling out a bottle of whiskey. He poured a small amount into a glass, then stepped to her side. "Drink this."

She was still gazing blindly at where he had stood a moment before, and tears spilled from her huge eyes to trail down her ashen cheeks. "Why did they do that?" she whispered. "Why did they blow up my apartment?"

Derek slid one big hand around her neck under her hair and then used the other to guide the glass to her lips, forcing her to take a healthy swallow of the whiskey. She choked and began coughing, but her eyes cleared of the dazed look. He put the glass in her hand. "Drink the rest," he ordered quietly.

Looking up at him, she obediently finished the whiskey, her faint grimace of distaste automatic. "I don't drink much," she told him softly.

He took the empty glass, a little startled to realize that his hand had remained on her neck beneath the warm curtain of her hair, that his fingers lightly stroked her satiny skin. He removed his hand slowly, very conscious of that soft skin, then stepped back and half turned away, fixing his attention on the coffee that was nearly ready.

"It was meant to kill me," she whispered.

He poured the coffee into two cups, adding whiskey to both. In a calm tone intended to keep her on balance, he asked, "You take cream and sugar, don't you?"

Shannon blinked. "Yes."

He fixed her coffee silently and handed her the cup: he picked up the cup he poured for himself, sipping it black. Watching her, he saw her wrinkle her nose at the taste of whiskey in her sweet coffee, but she sipped it slowly. He waited a few moments, until he was sure she was as calm as she could be under the circumstances, until the tears dried on her cheeks and a bit of color returned to her pale skin. "All right, Shannon. What happened next?"

She put her cup carefully on the counter beside her, then drew the blanket tighter around her body, looking steadily at him. "It all seemed so unreal. The apartment was on fire and the alarms were going off. People were rushing out of the building. I went too. Outside. And I knew it wasn't an accident. *I knew.* They'd put a bomb in the apartment. Then I heard someone running, and I saw a man coming toward me from across the street. He—I thought he had a gun. It looked like a gun. And he was looking at *me*, like he wanted to—his face was all twisted and furious. So I started running."

"He chased you?"

"Yes. I couldn't think. I wanted to call the police, but—"

"But what?"

Shannon bit her lip, then raised her chin and met his eyes steadily. "A few years ago, I worked for a company in another city. Some money disappeared from the office cash box, and I was accused of taking it." Her lips quivered slightly. "Nobody believed me. The police were sure I'd taken it, and my boss was sure. It was awful."

"What happened?" he asked softly.

"I was arrested. I couldn't afford bail. A few days before I would have gone to trial, another girl in the office was caught stealing money. They let me go."

But not, Derek realized, before a great deal of damage had been done to an innocent woman. He took a deep breath. "I see. So you were afraid that somehow this whole thing could have been blamed on you?"

"I don't know. I just couldn't call the police. I thought I'd gotten away from the man following me, but I wasn't sure. So I kept moving. For hours. I'd lost my purse and didn't have any money. I didn't dare go back to the apartment. And I was terrified to go to anyone I knew."

"Afraid they'd be in danger?"

"Yes."

"So you just kept moving until you thought of me?"

She nodded. "I was across town when I remembered what William had told me. It took a long time to find where you lived."

"I'm surprised you weren't arrested roaming the streets in that dress."

Shannon flushed vividly and drew the blanket tighter. "I hid every time I saw a patrol car. This—I don't usually dress like this, but my friend . . . this dress has a jacket, but I was carrying it when the apartment—"

"All right," he said gently, a little puzzled by her obvious discomfort with what was, definitely, a beautiful dress and one she wore extremely well. "I understand, Shannon. And you were smart not to go back to your apartment, or to anyone you knew. Considering how fast they moved to get you out of the way, I'd say we're up against pros."

"We?" Relief came into her expression. "You'll help me?"

In a light tone, he said, "I could never resist a lady in distress."

"I don't know how to thank you."

"Thanks may not be in order. We'd better wait and see if I can help. But first things first. You need to take a long, hot bath and then get some sleep."

"But—"

"It won't do either of us a bit of good if you wind up with pneumonia. You've been out in the cold for hours, you're exhausted, and you're in shock from what happened." He set his cup aside and moved to take her arm, easing her from the stool. "Come on, and don't argue with me. I know what I'm doing. Were you hurt?" he asked abruptly.

She flushed again, avoiding his steady gaze. "No. I limp because I was in an accident when I was a child."

Derek nodded, realizing quickly that she was very sensitive about the limp, which was undoubtedly much worse than usual after the night she had had. He led her through the apartment to the neat bathroom, turning on the light for her. "Have you eaten anything?"

She was gazing around, but looked back at him then, very small and pale in the engulfing blanket. "Not since lunch yesterday. But I couldn't—"

"You'll eat," he told her with calm certainty. "I'll go find something for you to wear, then fix an early breakfast. Make the water hot and soak until I tell you to get out."

For the first time, she smiled. "Yes, sir."

A bit unnerved by that smile, Derek rummaged in a linen cabinet and produced a bottle of bubble bath, looking at it with the baffled frown of a man who isn't quite sure where it came from. "Put some of this in," he instructed. "It's supposed to relax you."

Shannon nodded. "All right."

He backed out, shutting the door, and stood there a moment until he heard the water running. Then he went into his bedroom and found a flannel shirt and a pair of sweatpants with a drawstring waist. He carried them back to the bathroom and knocked briefly on the door before opening it a few inches and thrusting them inside. "Clothes," he called.

They were taken from his hand. "Thank you."

Derek closed the bathroom door and headed for the kitchen, tiredly rubbing the nape of his neck and wondering what in hell he'd gotten himself involved in this time.

She slid lower in the water, resting her head on the lip of the tub, and sighed without being aware of it. The lavender fragrance *was* soothing, and the hot water felt wonderful. The coldness was leaving her, seeping away, and with its leaving she became more aware of a steadily worsening pain. Automatically, she rubbed her aching hip, knowing she had badly overstrained the joint and her muscles. And he had noticed, of course. People always noticed. Especially men.

Shannon felt the warm trickle of tears escaping from the corners of her eyes, and made no move to wipe them away because she was too tired. *But you're alive, idiot!* Alive. How many times had people said that to her while she was growing up? You're alive. Be thankful. You could have been killed like your father. The leg brace is nothing, after all. What's a limp? At least you can walk.

So what if her apartment and every single thing she owned except the underwear she wore had gone up in smoke? She was alive. *So what if somebody's trying to kill you. . . .*

She wanted to draw herself into a small knot and pass unnoticed by the world. *And don't forget to turn your crippled hip to the wall!* she jeered silently at herself. Don't ever forget that, don't ever forget to hide the flaw. Wasn't that what her mother had told her over and over, even after the brace was gone and the limp a slight one? Walk straighter, Shannon. Wear a lift in your right shoe, Shannon, and never wear very high heels because they make you look awkward. Move slowly, Shannon. Hold your head up, Shannon. Look people in the eye, Shannon.

Years. Years of being gently told by the beautiful mother who couldn't bear imperfections that there was something wrong with her, something flawed. Years of submitting to the conspicuous matchmaking attempts of her mother, and of watching the dutiful boys and, later, men avoiding any glance at her leg. And, finally, escape to a life of her own, only to discover painfully that there was still something wrong with her. That men still avoided glances at her leg and never asked her to dance, even though she could because of her mother's determined lessons.

And she hadn't told Derek Ross all of it. She hadn't told him that Civatech had been her fourth job in as many years. She hadn't told him that after that first devastating job two more had been lost because she wasn't perfect, because she limped. Because she was a lame duck in a world of swans.

Stop it! she told herself. She was healthy. Alive. Even if somebody was trying to kill her. A giggle escaped her, and Shannon opened her eyes to stare fixedly up at the ceiling. She was getting hysterical, dammit. Tired. She was just tired, that was all, that was all it was. And so sleepy. The bath was making her sleepy. Her eyes slowly closed again, and disjointed images whirled behind her lids.

He was such a big man, she thought drowsily. He made her feel safe. Made her feel, for the first time in many long years, that she . . . that maybe . . . her hip throbbed and ached. She rubbed it harder, the growing pain of it fighting off drowsiness. It hurt, and she was just too tired to tell herself it didn't. Her muscles, sustaining their strength as long as possible, had finally given in; they twitched in painful spasms, knotting, making her entire leg tremble, jerk. And the joint felt raw and hot, hurting until she bit her lip.

"Shannon?" He knocked softly on the door.

She swallowed hard. "Yes?"

"Breakfast in ten minutes."

"All right."

She pulled herself from the tub and let the water out while she was drying off. Any weight at all on her right leg was almost unbearable now, and it was difficult for her to draw on the sweatpants. Even sitting down hurt. She finally got the pants on and tied the drawstring, trying to find some amusement in the extremely baggy fit. The flannel shirt was also ridiculously large: she rolled up the sleeves over her forearms and thought idly that she certainly made a fetching sight.

She left her things in the bathroom and moved toward the kitchen, gritting her teeth in order to walk. *Hold your head up, Shannon. Move slowly, Shannon. Walk straighter, Shannon. And, for God's sake, look people in the eye!*

She looked Derek in the eye as she entered the small kitchen, and he instantly came to help her to the breakfast bar, supporting her totally. "Here, sit down. What have you done to yourself?" he asked roughly.

Shannon blinked back tears as he eased her onto a padded stool at the bar. Fooling no one, as usual, she thought tiredly. "I'm all right," she murmured. "I'm just not used to so much walking. The bath helped."

He looked down at her with a frown, then went to pour coffee, and set the cup and a plate containing an omelet before her. "Eat." He fixed his own coffee and carried it and his plate to the bar, sitting across from her. "How did you hurt your leg?" he asked bluntly.

Shannon was looking fixedly at her plate, trying to eat enough to satisfy him although she hurt too much to feel hunger. "A car accident when I was four," she answered, a little relieved by his open notice of her flaw. At least he wasn't tactfully avoiding the subject.

"Is it the leg or the hip?" he asked in a casual tone.

She stole a glance at his face and found it intent but relaxed, the dark eyes gentle. He had put on a shirt, she realized vaguely, a dark sweatshirt that set off his blond handsomeness and made her disturbingly aware of him. "Both," she said finally. "They thought I'd lose the leg for a while, but I didn't."

"You shouldn't have been wearing those heels," he told her, not in criticism, but understanding. "High heels throw the hips forward and the spine out of alignment. It *looks* sexy as hell, mind you, but I've noticed that fashion tends to put women in uncomfortable clothes and shoes most of the time. And it's worse for you because of your hip."

Shannon found a smile from somewhere despite the fire in her hip. Other than the friend who had bullied her into agreeing to go to the party last night, no one had ever talked to her so matter-of-factly about her flaw—especially not a man. Men tended to avoid any mention at all of her leg. She ate most of the omelet, more to please him than anything else, trying to keep her mind off the worsening pain.

When she had finally laid her fork aside, Derek reached a long arm to the counter, getting a bottle of pills she hadn't noticed until then. He shook one small white pill into his palm and held it out to her. "This is for pain. It's mild, but I couldn't give it to you on an empty stomach. Take it."

She looked at him, hesitant even though she realized that the pain had brought tears to her eyes again.

"It's all right, Shannon."

After a moment, she took the pill and swallowed it with coffee. *He has the eyes of an old soul. So wise.* She trusted him without even wondering why she did. She had almost literally put her life in his hands, after all.

Derek rose from his stool and came around to her, bending to gather her into his arms.

She was startled: her voice emerged breathless as she said, "You don't have to—"

"Yes, I do," he said calmly, handling her slight weight very easily and very gently. "You're in agony every time you move; you've overstrained your hip with all that walking, and it's getting even with you. Now, shut up," he added politely, "and relax."

Shannon felt very small and very confused, but her arms had automatically encircled his neck and she shut up. He carried her through the apartment to his dark bedroom, laying her very gently in the center of the rumpled bed. Before she had realized what he was going to do, he rolled her smoothly onto her left side so that she was facing away from him, and she felt the bed give as he sat on it.

"What—"

"Shhh." One big hand rubbed the small of her back in a soothing rhythm, and the other came to rest on her aching hip. "Don't worry," he said quietly. "I was a masseur in a former life. Close your eyes, Shannon." The hand on her hip moved gently and surely, and when the pain almost instantly lessened Shannon was so surprised that she relaxed.

"You must have been a good one."

"Better?"

"Yes." She drew a shuddering breath. "Much better."

"Good. The pill will take effect soon, and you'll sleep for a good long time. When you wake up, we'll talk about what to do next, all right?"

"Mmmm." She didn't even notice when he smoothed the tail of the flannel shirt up to her waist so that only the thin material of the sweatpants separated her flesh from his gentle touch. She was aware only of his soothing hands and the magic of them. "Where did you get the pills?"

"From my doctor." He rubbed her hip slowly, very conscious that the back of her thigh pressed warmly against his hip. "I wrenched my shoulder a while back. And you're supposed to be trying to sleep."

She laughed sleepily, completely relaxed now in the darkness. He was a warlock, that's what he was. "I know. Why are you being so kind to me, Derek? You shouldn't be kind to me. I'm a lot of trouble."

"Are you?" He kept his voice soft, aware that she was almost asleep and hardly knew what she was saying.

"Oh, yes." She moved a little under his hands, like a cat shifting lazily to find the sun.

"How are you trouble?" He moved both hands to her hip, then slid one down over her thigh, his sure, steady touch easing the muscles that were in spasm.

"Things happen to me," she said, sighing with contentment as her taut leg relaxed slowly and the ache in her hip faded to a dull throb she hardly felt. "I'm bad luck, just bad luck, always. That money . . . and then William . . . and now somebody's trying to kill me."

She had relaxed totally under his touch, and Derek knew she was asleep. He gazed down at her, his hands still massaging gently for long moments until he was sure she was deeply asleep. Then his hands went still—but didn't leave her.

She was, he thought, like a beautiful, fragile bird with a badly mended wing. Somebody had once—or many times—told her she could never fly again, and she was completely convinced that it was true. It was in her eyes, her haunted eyes, that she felt she had an open wound that would never heal.

Derek drew away slowly and rose from the bed, bending to pull the covers up over her. He straightened and stood looking down at her in the gloom, dawn's light struggling through the curtains. Then he silently and swiftly left the room. In the den, he turned on the television low, intending to see if there were early news reports of the explosion at Shannon's apartment building. He sat on the couch and lighted a cigarette, staring broodingly at the television screen.

God, he was tired. The situation in Algeria had nearly turned into a fiasco despite his best efforts, and getting out of the country after everything hit the fan hadn't been fun. Add to that too many long hours in a drafty, noisy cargo plane and a bare four hours' sleep before Shannon's predawn arrival at his door, and "exhausted" was merely a mildly descriptive word with little relevance to his condition.

And that was why, of course. That was why he'd felt so unutterably moved when she had met his gaze in the kitchen, her own big gentle eyes suffering silently. That was why his chest had ached intolerably and something inside it throbbed with a feeling it had never known.

Oh, yes, he was tired. Tired enough to wonder why certain parts of his body didn't know about tired. Tired enough that he still felt her body beneath his touch, branded in his mind. Tired enough that he wanted to return to the bedroom and crawl in beside her, hold her, feel her naked against him.

Derek swore softly. She was lost, alone, in shock and pain, and he wanted to . . . of course he wanted to. And if he found that Shannon wasn't alone, that there was a lover in the wings somewhere whom she carefully hadn't drawn into danger while she had roamed the streets last night, lost and desperately afraid, he would very probably tear the poor bastard limb from limb.

But she had come to him for help, and that was the important thing, no matter how he felt. Few knew better than he that the situation between them was tailor-made for the right kind of emotions sparked for all the wrong reasons. All her defenses—assuming she had any—were down, splintered around her. And even without the threats against her, Derek was all too aware that she was a fragile woman, a hurt woman.

And with that wounded spirit threatened by faceless people for enigmatic reasons, she was even more vulnerable, more fragile. She was lost and he was her lifeline; if he moved too quickly, that delicate thread binding them together would snap, and once that happened it could never be repaired.

He stubbed out his cigarette and sat up straighter,

leaning forward to catch the drone of the television as the early news came on and the scene shifted almost immediately to a gutted apartment in a building across town. He watched carefully, listening intently to the reporter's statement that the fire marshals had found evidence of arson, in fact, of an explosive device. No one had been hurt in the blast and resulting fire, but a tenant was missing. Police were searching for the missing tenant, Shannon Brown, whom they wanted for questioning.

Derek sat back and glanced at his watch. He wondered how early he could phone the governor.

Two

"You're sure she's all right?" William Franklin's voice had lost the last vestiges of sleep, and he sounded worried as hell.

"I'm sure. She's asleep in my bed right now."

There was a beat of silence, and then the governor's voice came over the telephone line more calmly. "I knew you'd look after her if anything happened."

"Uh-huh. And you knew something would happen, didn't you? That's why you gave her my name. Is there anything you'd like to tell me, Governor?"

"Stop being so damed formal," Franklin ordered peevishly. "You're beginning to sound like a government operative, and heaven knows you never have before."

Derek took a deep breath and let it out very slowly. "William, my doorbell rang at four this morning, and I found a very frightened, very vulnerable lady on my doorstep. I'm functioning on about four hours' sleep, I have a monumental case of jet lag, a pounding headache, and what I suspect is the beginning of a hellish problem. Play games with me, and I'm coming over there to tear your heart out."

Franklin chuckled. "Now you sound like yourself."

"William."

"All right, all right. Just remember this: You take care of that lady. She's something special."

"I caught that. Why's she special to you?" A blunt question, but Derek was a blunt man.

Calmly, Franklin said, "Partly because she took a bullet meant for me."

"What?"

"You heard me. There was a private party about two years ago for my key campaign workers. Some maniac decided to kill me, and Shannon saw what none of the security people did. She threw herself at me, knocked me down. I didn't get hit, but she did, in the shoulder."

Slowly, Derek said, "There was no publicity."

"No."

Derek decided not to ask how that had been arranged: as it was, he knew more than he cared to about "political realities." "I see. That's why you got her a job at Civatech?"

"One of the reasons. While she was recovering from the wound, Annie and I also grew very fond of her." Franklin hesitated, then asked, "Have you ever met someone who'd been slapped down so many times they'd learned to expect another slap?"

"Yes." Derek cleared his throat. "At four this morning."

Franklin sighed. "It's obvious, isn't it? That damned limp and some bad luck, and the poor kid's convinced she's just taking up valuable space in the world. Sometimes she forgets it all. And then she remembers, and it's like watching a flower close up."

After a moment, Derek said, "So tell me about Civatech."

"Not much I can tell you." Franklin accepted the shift in subject. "Shannon could probably tell you a lot, even more than she realizes she knows. She's observant and perceptive. All I know is that some of those odd sentences she picked out of a few letters sounded suspiciously like the codes I remember from my Army days. And with a high-security firm like Civatech, I just had to wonder."

Derek told him what Shannon had reported to her supervisor about the nonexistent product and the nonexistent company. "What do you think?"

Worried, Franklin said, "Dammit, I don't know. Some of their *products* are not exactly nice toys. If a design was scrapped, it was probably because there was something that made it unworkable, uncontrollable, therefore, quite dangerous. If some idiot has built a prototype from a defective design and means to peddle it to the highest bidder— Damn, I can—"

"No, you stay out of it. If something happens and I think I'll need your clout, I'll let you know. Civatech is a private company with a lot of military contracts; we should keep you out of this, if possible. I'll protect Shannon while I do some checking. I know a few sources."

Reluctantly, Franklin said, "If you say so. But keep me advised. And, if something goes wrong, Derek—"

"If something goes wrong," Derek said steadily, "I'll see to it that Shannon gets to you safely."

"All right." The governor's voice was somber. "Take care. And take care of her."

"I will." Derek cradled the receiver and then ran a hand round the back of his neck. The first thing he had to do, he acknowledged, was to get some sleep, otherwise he wouldn't be worth the bullet to shoot him. He looked at his watch, calculating that between the pill and her exhaustion Shannon probably would sleep at least another six hours. Trusting that she had indeed lost her pursuer of the night before, he stretched out on the couch and mentally set his internal clock to wake him up.

Then he went to sleep. All of him did, except the watchful part that never slept.

Across the street, a tall man who had stood with utter stillness in the shadows of waning night and the chill of a gray dawn straightened as the street became active with the bustle of day. He stepped out of the alley where he had waited so watchfully for several hours and strolled casually across the street, into the lobby of the apartment building that had been the focus of his attention.

There was a row of mailboxes in one wall, and he stood scanning them intently, his peculiarly colorless eyes coming to rest at last on a single name. One brow lifted and he whistled softly, tonelessly. He reached up to tap a knuckle against the nameplate thoughtfully, then glanced toward the stairs. After a silent debate, not one argument of which showed on his expressionless face, he turned away and retraced his steps.

He didn't pause at the alley this time, but moved along briskly, nothing setting him apart from other pedestrians . . . except that those other early-morning people sent the tall man unconsciously wary glances and instinctively gave him plenty of room on the sidewalk. He didn't notice or, if he did, found nothing unusual in the reaction.

He hailed a cab at the end of the block, changing taxis three times before finally reaching his destination. And, even then, he waited across the street, watching the traffic pass for nearly an hour before he strolled over and entered a second apartment building, this one more shabby than the first. He ignored the elevator, taking the stairs and climbing to the third floor, knocking lightly on the door of a corner apartment. It opened for him almost instantly, and he went inside.

"Well?" she asked tensely.

"The girl found sanctuary," he said a bit dryly.

"What? With who?"

"Whom," he murmured.

She frowned at him, her thin little face angry. "Stop correcting my grammar!" Like him, she had no accent of any kind, but a perceptive observer would have realized that neither of them had spoken English from childhood. "She got away from them? Where did she go?"

"To our old friend from Prague."

She caught her breath, and a flush came and went quickly on her small face. "Him? But he was out of the country, you said—"

"It appears he has returned."

"How did she know to go to him?"

"I have no idea. She went directly to his apartment after checking a telephone directory, so I assume she knew who she was going to." He shrugged out of his coat and went into the kitchen, returning with a cup of coffee. "It is difficult to judge," he went on thoughtfully, "how much or how little she may know. However, since they destroyed her apartment, it is reasonable to assume she knows something."

"And so?"

"We wait."

Shannon was still sleeping when Derek woke exactly six hours later. He checked on her and then went to take a shower. The rest had done little more than take the edge off his weariness, but he was accustomed to much less sleep during an assignment and tended to be grateful for what he could get. He felt almost human after showering and shaving, more so after hot coffee, and by the second cup was able to think more clearly than he had during the small hours of the morning.

The most important thing was Shannon's safety, which meant that he had to discover who was after her and why. He could do a little basic research from his apartment by making a few calls, but sooner or later he'd have to do some reconnoitering at Civatech and find out just what was going on there. And Shannon would have to be with him, since he wasn't about to leave her alone if he could help it. She'd be safe enough with William, but Derek felt uneasy for several reasons when he considered that alternative.

Since they had moved so quickly to get Shannon, and since they had not even bothered to make the explosion look like an accident, Derek had to assume they were both nervous and unaware of her closeness to the governor. If they had not been nervous, the explosion would certainly have appeared accidental, and if they had realized just how close to William she actually was, they might have hesitated to go after her at all. It was public knowledge that William Franklin was a good friend and a very bad enemy, and he was hardly the type to keep quiet if someone he cared about was hurt or killed.

However, now that they had indeed tried to kill Shannon, it was extremely doubtful they'd give up on that intention, even if they chanced to find out about her relationship with William. As Derek had told him on the phone, he was their ace in the hole, a considerable amount of clout in an emergency, so Derek was reluctant to hide Shannon away in the governor's mansion unless it was absolutely necessary.

He poured more coffee and stared down at the breakfast bar where the morning paper lay, still neatly folded; he'd remembered to get it from the hallway, but hadn't read it. He lighted a cigarette, frowning down at the paper without really seeing it. Shannon and he probably didn't have much time, he was thinking. Since there was no past or present connection between him and Shannon, it was reasonable to assume she would be safe with him. Except for one small thing.

Who he was. There weren't twenty people—counting Shannon and the Franklins—in Richmond, Virginia, who knew who and what Derek Ross was; the bad thing was that a good fifteen of the twenty wore black hats. If the people at Civatech had "street" connections and knew the right questions to ask, it would only be a matter of time before someone alerted them that a government agent known on both sides of the street as something of an outlaw lived in the city. They'd check him out automatically as a possible danger, and since he had long ago learned that anyone could be found if the search were careful enough and professional enough, he rarely bothered to hide his whereabouts behind unlisted phones or assumed names. So he would be easy to find.

Shannon wouldn't be safe here for much longer.

That was something Derek acknowledged and accepted. So they'd have to leave soon. Which meant Shannon had to have clothes; she'd stand out far too much wearing his too-large clothing, and even if it were safe to return to her apartment, he doubted there was anything left there to salvage. The problem was, Derek didn't want to leave her alone, nor was he ready to endanger her by taking her out in public, at least until he had a better idea of what was going on at Civatech.

Absently, he unfolded the paper and began scanning the headlines, wondering if there was anyone who could—his glance caught and held on a photo, and his eyes sharpened as he read the caption and the accompanying short article. "Well, well," he murmured thoughtfully. "Nice of Lady Luck to help me out."

The phone directory was equally helpful, and he placed a call to a rather well-known hotel in the city. Unsurprised, he waited patiently while he was switched from one person to another, perfectly aware that he was working his way progressively through the layers of careful security that tended to surround wealthy and famous people. It took a good ten minutes to reach the center of all that protection, and when he did he commented a bit dryly, "I'd have found it easier to reach the President."

A warm chuckle came from the line. "Derek, it's good to hear from you! Sorry about the gauntlet, but Zach insists. He's gotten even more protective, especially the last couple of months."

Soberly, Derek said, "Yes, Kelsey told me about Teddy. How is she, Raven?"

Sighing, Raven Long said, "Physically, recovered. Emotionally is something else. She and Zach really wanted that baby."

"Tell them both how sorry I am, will you?"

"Of course." Her voice lightened. "What are you doing in Richmond?"

"I live here."

"Oh?" She laughed. "Well, how could I know? You had a flat in London, a place in Hong Kong, and—what was that? A chateau in France?"

"A very small chateau. I also have an apartment in Richmond."

"Any port in a storm," she murmured.

Her tone was rather deliberately gentle, and Derek chuckled. "Heard about Algeria, have you?"

"I have very good ears."

"I'll say," he observed dryly.

"You made a big bang over there," she explained. "For someone who scorns firearms, you tend to make a lot of noise sometimes." Before he could comment, she was going on briskly, "By my calculation, you should have just barely returned from there, and even iron men have to sleep. So why are you awake when you should be blissfully unconscious?"

Derek grinned. That was Raven—right to the crux of the matter. "I need a favor," he told her.

"Oh, good, I was hoping you did." Her voice was cheerful now. "Josh and Zach are busy with a union strike, and since they claim I'd be a distraction at the bargaining table I've been sitting here twiddling my thumbs."

"A waste of your vast talents," he agreed solemnly.

She made a rude noise. "Never mind the editorial comments, just tell me what you want."

"I need you to do a little shopping for me."

"Anything interesting?" she inquired hopefully.

"Ladies' wear."

Raven laughed. "Get your story ready, pal, because *this* I've got to hear. Sizes and colors, please."

And Derek, who had a good eye for such things and who had also checked the clothing Shannon had left in the bathroom, recited sizes, suggested colors, and gave her his address. "From the skin out," he finished, then added hastily before she could comment on *that*, "It's possible this building is under surveillance, so act accordingly."

"Good heavens," she said, but not as if the prospect of trouble daunted her.

In fact, she sounded rather pleased, and Derek said severely, "You're not in this, understand? I know that gang of yours loves trouble, but if you all come in on this I'll have Hagen on my back and that's the last thing I need."

Without responding, she said casually, "Where is the maestro of stealth and deceit, by the way? We haven't heard from him lately."

"Last I knew, he was foaming at the mouth

because some smart lady had ruined one of his plans. I think she snuck out the back door while he was sauntering in the front."

After a moment, Raven said slowly, "Her name wouldn't be Sara, would it?"

"I don't know. Friend of yours?"

"In absentia," Raven answered in a distracted tone. "I think maybe our Sarah should check on that; if that son of a worm is hounding the poor girl. . ." Briskly, she said, "I'll get the clothes, Derek, and be at your place as soon as possible."

He didn't ask questions. "Great. And, Raven —thanks."

But she had already hung up. She was like that, he reflected, cradling his own receiver. She helped automatically because she didn't know any other way to be.

Lady Luck had gifted him with a number of friends like that.

Shannon knew as soon as she opened her eyes that she had slept a long time; a glance at the clock on the nightstand confirmed the feeling. It was late in the afternoon. It was also not her nightstand.

She sat up, staring around the bedroom that wasn't hers either. This wasn't her plain little room with its colorless pseudo-oak furniture, shabby drapes, and bland carpet. This was a larger room with heavy drapes and deep carpet, and the furniture was dark and massive and obviously not pseudo anything.

Frowning, she looked down to see the very large flannel shirt and baggy sweatpants she was wearing. Also not hers. Then, even as she pushed back her tousled hair and swung her legs from the large bed, she remembered.

Civatech. The explosion. An eternally long night of walking, frightened, in pain, alone. And then finding a big, tough, blond man with wonderful dark eyes who had listened to her, fed her, put her to bed, and rubbed her aching hip until the pain went away and she could sleep.

Shannon drew a deep breath and rose to her bare feet, relieved to find that her hip was stiff but not hurting. She went to the closed door, eased it open, and heard the murmur of voices from the den. Biting her lip, she hesitated, then slipped from the room and moved toward the sound.

There were two people in the den. Derek was standing, leaning his hands on the back of a chair while he talked. He was dressed in dark slacks and a gray shirt, and looked more handsome than she remembered. On the couch was a woman, and Shannon instantly became aware of her own disheveled hair, baggy clothing, and bare feet: this woman probably always had that effect on other women. Her long black hair gleamed almost blue and was worn casually in a ponytail high on her head. Her face was striking, not perfect or even particularly beautiful, but somehow lovely and unforgettable. She had wide, merry violet eyes and a warm smile—directed at Derek, at the moment. She was dressed simply in slacks and a silk blouse, a single gold chain at her throat, but she could have worn the same outfit to a diplomatic ball, and no one would have considered her underdressed. Style. The lady had style.

Another swan, Shannon thought miserably.

"Shannon." Derek came to meet her, and his dark eyes searched her face. "Feeling better?"

She nodded. "Yes, thank you." Her voice was soft and toneless, without expression.

He frowned fleetingly as he took her arm lightly and guided her to the couch, introducing her to Raven Long. Then, when she sat down, he said, "I'll get you some coffee," and briskly left the room.

"It seems you've had a rough time," Raven said, looking at her gravely.

"He—he told you?"

"He told me. We worked together in the past."

Shannon looked at her, unwilling to acknowledge how relieved she felt because she had just noticed that the other woman wore a gold wedding band. "I see."

Raven gestured to a stack of boxes on the floor by the couch. "He didn't want to leave you alone, and since your clothes went up in smoke, he asked me to get a few things for you." She studied the other woman, ignoring her suddenly flushed face. "The sizes should be about right, I think, and he was on the mark with colors."

A bit unsteadily, Shannon said, "I don't know how to thank you. But I'll pay you back—"

Raven smiled at her warmly. "You don't worry about that, all right? Time enough later for the unimportant things." She would have told Shannon to forget the debt entirely, but she was all too aware that this woman would find gifts difficult to accept; she was a hurt person, and hurt people clung to pride. "First, we have to get those creeps off your back—"

"Take yourself out of that *we*," Derek said firmly,

returning to the room and placing a cup of coffee on the table before Shannon. "I told you, you aren't involved, Raven."

She smiled at him.

"I mean it," he insisted, sinking down in a chair. "Josh would have my head on a platter, and Zach would serve it to him!"

"I told you, they're busy." She looked at Shannon, explaining, "My husband and a friend of ours."

"They wouldn't be busy long," Derek said, "if you got involved in this. Not, at least, with a union strike. They'd be busy either taking me apart or else getting hip-deep in the situation themselves. No, Raven."

She shook her head. "Still an outlaw."

"I earned the name," he agreed dryly.

Shannon looked from one to the other, puzzled, and Raven explained after smiling, again. "Derek doesn't like other people's rules. He's infamous for his ability to go into tricky situations without backup and come out with his skin intact . . . and with whatever he went in *after.* He also— though he'd die rather than admit it—spins some of the most intricate tactical webs it's ever been my pleasure to see, resulting in whole governments at each other's throats by the time he waltzes out of their countries."

"That's enough," Derek said mildly.

Raven was still smiling, and her eyes were alight. "Shannon should know what she's gotten herself into. She should know that you despise guns and don't know karate from chop suey, which makes the rest of us wonder how on earth you've managed to stay alive this long."

"I throw a mean punch," Derek murmured.

"He does that," Raven told Shannon. "He also swims like a fish, has eyes like a cat, and if you dropped him in the middle of a desert he'd find the only oasis within a fifty-mile radius in under an hour. He never gets lost or ruffled, never walks a straight line if he can find a curve or an angle, and never, *never* gives up."

"The queue to pay homage forms to the right," Derek told Shannon dryly.

Raven grinned at him. "Hey, pal, I started that line years ago. I think it was when you saved me from having to say 'comrade' whenever I addressed someone."

"Just because I thought it'd be a shame to hide all that hair underneath a babushka," he told her.

Shannon was staring at Raven. "You mean—?"

Cheerful, Raven said, "If Derek hadn't had such good instincts, I would have been grabbed by a double agent and taken to the other side as a prize."

Shannon turned her gaze to Derek. "I don't think I really believed it until now," she said wonderingly. "It all seemed so unreal."

He looked at her for a moment, then said, "Why don't you go try on the clothes Raven brought. I may have been wrong on the sizes, and we might have to exchange something."

Obediently, Shannon gathered the boxes and carried them into his bedroom, closing the door softly behind her. Derek lighted a cigarette, frowning, while Raven watched him.

Usually, Derek smoked in a lazy, almost careless manner. He would frown critically at smoke ring after smoke ring, searching, he said, for the perfect one. It was not an affectation, but a subtle and deliberate bit of sleight of hand; anyone watching tended to pay attention to what he was doing, which left him free to observe what was going on around him without seeming to look at all.

Lacking Kelsey's inborn chameleon gifts, Derek had mastered several subtle sleight of hand distractions in body language, and used each so skillfully that only another agent or actor would have noticed.

Raven, a former agent and innate actress, noticed. She also noticed that Derek was smoking now in a quick, hard manner that was not at all deceptive. "Worried, pal?"

He leaned his fair head back against the chair and stared at the ceiling. "You weren't followed?"

"No. And there wasn't a hint of anyone watching this place. Combat jitters?"

The phrase was common among agents and referred to something that might have been instinct or intuition; a good agent could often sense the seemingly eternal moment right before everything hit the fan—as Derek had in England years before.

He shrugged a little. "No, not that. I just wonder what it's all *about*. What's so important that they moved that quickly to get Shannon out of the way permanently, and simply because she noticed some puzzling phrases in a few letters? Why not give her an unexpected holiday and keep an eye on her, or hire a couple of dumb gunsels to grab her and hold her incommunicado for a while?"

"Maybe she knows more than she's aware of, enough so that they couldn't take any chances."

"Then we're talking about something very big involving some very ruthless people." He sighed roughly. "Dammit."

After a moment, Raven gathered her handbag and rose to her feet. "You weren't wrong on the sizes, so I'll be leaving. I promised Josh I'd come straight back," she added absently.

Since he knew Josh Long, Derek grimaced. "That doesn't sound like him," he said, putting his cigarette out in an ashtray on a table beside the chair. "Is there something you haven't told me?"

Raven waved him back when he would have gotten up, then turned toward the door. She didn't answer until her hand was on the knob, then paused to look back at him. "Nothing at all," she lied easily, smiling at him. "Call if you need anything, pal. Anything, no matter what. If you need a safe house, Long Enterprises has a warehouse or two in the city, and I've a friend in Europe at the moment who offered his loft. Just let me know." Then she slipped out of the apartment.

Derek stared after her for a moment, then rose and paced restlessly over to the window. He didn't see Raven leave the building, but he hadn't expected to; she was too good to make her exit obvious even to him. He studied the street below, then scanned the building across the street. His gaze came to rest finally on the narrow entrance to a dark alley. A good place from which to watch. But, hell, there was always a good place somewhere.

He sighed and turned away from the window. Impossible to predict the turn of every card. Had Shannon lost her pursuer of the night before?

Probably. Did the people who were after her know where she was? Unlikely. Not yet, at least. Were there a couple of wild cards in the deal, fate's giggle at them all? Who knew? Anything was possible.

"Is she gone?"

He had been standing in the center of the den looking at nothing. At the sound of Shannon's hesitant voice, he focused on her where she stood just inside the room. "Yes. She had to get back."

Raven's taste in clothes, he reflected, was right on target. And his suggestion of colors had been perfect as well. Warm colors, he had said, reds and golds and creamy browns; no cool blues or greens. Shannon was wearing ivory-colored slacks belted at her small waist, with a red silk blouse, full-sleeved and tightly cuffed at the wrists.

"She even got shoes," Shannon said a little breathlessly, looking down at the toes of her cream-colored pumps. Then she looked back at Derek, unable to read his still face and dark eyes. "Everything fits. It's . . . it's too much, though. She got several outfits and sleepwear and—and everything. Even a hairbrush. I don't know how to thank both of you for helping me like this. I'll never be able to repay you. I'll try, though, I'll—"

"Shannon."

She bit her lip. "What?"

"You're beautiful."

Shannon felt as if someone had kicked the breath out of her, and her heart thudded. He was just standing there, hands in his pockets, looking at her steadily. Simply being nice, of course, he was simply being nice because he had kind eyes, infinitely understanding eyes, the eyes of an old soul.

"Thank you," she whispered, because it was the right thing to say.

He smiled. "You don't believe me." It was a curiously gentle, chiding statement.

Her eyes skittered away from his, but her chin lifted. "There are mirrors. I know what I look like."

Derek shook his head. "No, you don't. Someone cracked your mirror a long time ago, and now that's the one you carry with you all the time, the only one you look into."

She gave him a baffled glance and moved uneasily toward the couch. Why did he keep looking at her like that? And why was he talking about mirrors? She knew all about mirrors. A lifetime of mirrors. "Shouldn't we be talking about Civatech?" She sat down and sipped her lukewarm coffee.

"I've put out a few feelers," he murmured. "There isn't much we can do until I get a response."

Shannon was carefully not looking at him, although she could feel his gaze. "Feelers? You mean you called someone?"

"A couple of friends in the high-tech business. The scientific community likes to gossip as well as the rest of us, and failures are a prime topic."

"Failures?"

"You said it was a supposedly scrapped design."

"Oh." She nodded nervously. "Yes, of course. Then you believe your friends may have heard of the design?"

"It's a possibility worth checking into. Shannon, are you afraid of me?"

Startled, she looked up at him. "Afraid of you?" There was astonishment in her voice, and it occurred to her only then that he was a man many would be afraid of. Odd. She had felt no fear of him at all, not even in those first tense moments. She trusted him without even thinking about it. "No. I—I'm not afraid of you."

"Do you trust me?"

"Yes." She tried to lessen the importance of that instant response by adding defensively, "William does, after all."

Derek nodded slightly. He was still standing in the middle of the room, hands in his pockets as he watched her intently. "I may have to ask you to trust me unconditionally. Will you be able to do that, Shannon?"

"What do you mean, unconditionally?"

"Just that. No reservations, no hesitations. If I tell you to do something, you have to do it—no matter what. Our lives could depend on it."

Shannon was afraid now, but not of him. "I don't understand."

"We'll be leaving here in a day or two; it won't be safe to stay longer." His voice was calm, steady. "They don't know you're with me, but if they know the right people to ask they'll find out I'm a possible threat. So we'll have to keep moving. I know a few places, safe at least for a while. But the important thing is that you have to trust me. We may have to move very quickly, with no warning."

"All right," she said steadily.

He smiled. "No hesitation?"

"What choice do I have?"

"True." He stopped smiling.

"I'm sorry." Suddenly she wanted to cry. "I shouldn't have said that. You took in a stranger, and you didn't have to. You didn't have to be so kind or decide to get involved in this mess—"

"Shannon?"

She put her cup down, wondering why she'd been holding it, then met his gaze. "What?"

"You're beautiful."

The two simple words had the same impact on her this time; she couldn't breathe and her heart thumped heavily. "Stop saying that," she managed to say.

"Unconditional trust, remember?"

The room was suddenly getting small, very small, until she thought she could reach out and touch the walls, stand up and bump her head on the ceiling. It was small, and full of him, and she couldn't look away from those dark eyes. Her throat was tense, tight, and her shaking fingers twined together in her lap.

He just *stood* there, just stood there waiting, as if he were prepared to wait forever if that's how long it took her to answer. Her hands were cold and there wasn't any space at all between her and him, he filled it somehow, made it thick somehow with emotions she didn't understand.

"Stop it," she whispered, not even sure what she was asking him to stop.

"No." His voice remained calm, his face still, and he made no move toward her. "This is important, Shannon. You carry a cracked mirror around with you long enough, and everything begins to show a distorted reflection. You have to see what's there—beginning with your own true reflection."

"I can't—"

"I know you can't. Not yet. That's why you have to trust me to see for you until you learn how. Do you trust me to do that?"

She stared at him, somehow aware that this

was important, and not because she needed to believe she was beautiful. It was important, she realized, because her trust in Derek did indeed have to be absolute. If she doubted him in any way, hesitated to believe anything he said, her own indecision could conceivably put them both in greater danger.

Her head understood that, but her heart . . . how could anyone trust that completely? And she had known him barely twelve hours, knew so little about him.

"Trust me, Shannon." His voice was softer now, deeper, and curiously compelling. "Trust me to tell you the truth always, no matter what. You're beautiful."

"I limp." It was an automatic response, her greatest doubt given voice.

"No, you don't."

What was the matter with him, was he blind? Of course she limped, she wouldn't deny reality! No one could trust that much, no one at all!

"You don't limp. Last night you did, because you were exhausted and you'd strained your hip. Today you're walking with no sign of a limp. It isn't something that's always with you, Shannon, and no one sees it but you. A part of that distorted reflection."

Was it possible? No, no, her mother would have told her. Her mother would have—and then she remembered her friend Janie, she of the red dress and gentle bullying.

"*You only limp when you're thinking about it, Shannon, or when you're tired. Half that limp's in your mind—and in your mother's!*"

"Mother says I limp," she whispered, remembering. Remembering her last visit, when her mother had scolded her gently for not walking slowly enough.

"Then her mirror is cracked too," Derek told her softly. "You were hurt once, and she can't forget it. That doesn't mean she's right, Shannon. I'm right. Trust me."

Shannon stared into those quiet dark eyes, those infinitely wise eyes, and the room was small again, so small she could barely breathe. And despite that closeness, or because of it, she suddenly felt as if something heavy had been lifted away from her.

"All right." It was said on a sigh.

"You're beautiful, Shannon." He was smiling.

She squared her shoulders and lifted her chin, and this time she said it not because it was the thing to say, but because she meant it.

"Thank you."

Three

They remained in his apartment the rest of the afternoon and evening, and if some hurdle had been cleared by his insistence on absolute trust and her conscious surrender to that, something else had happened as well. Shannon couldn't really put her finger on it except to realize that she was more aware of him now, more alert to his every movement, his glances, his smile. As if, by declaring her trust, she had thrust aside the wary veil that people inevitably hid behind in the presence of a stranger.

The odd thing was that she felt Derek had not thrust his veil aside simply because he never hung one between himself and other people. She was seeing him clearly, but she knew instinctively that he had seen her that way from the first. Maybe it was his eyes, she thought, those tolerant, ancient eyes. Maybe his old soul had outgrown the need for disguises and veils.

"You look bemused." He sat down beside her on the couch, his expression quizzical.

Dinner, efficiently prepared by him, was over and the apartment was quiet except for the soft semiclassical music coming from his stereo. Shannon felt . . . peculiar. Her throat was tight and her heart thudded unevenly, and she had a mad impulse to reach out and touch his gleaming blond hair. She looked fixedly down at her hands, folded together in her lap, wondering what was wrong with her.

"Shannon?"

If it were possible to bottle his voice, she thought distractedly, somebody could make a million bucks selling the stuff to airlines and hospitals; it would instantly reassure passengers and patients that nothing bad could ever happen. Ever. "I was just thinking that you—have an old soul." *Oh, great, Shannon, now the man's going to think you're a flake!*

"Sometimes it feels that way."

She looked at him hesitantly, discovering that he was watching her with no sign of amusement on his hard, handsome face. "I meant—"

"I know what you meant." He smiled. "Maybe it's true. I've always liked to believe we're given the chance to correct the mistakes we make."

"And be rewarded for the things we do right?"

He shrugged. "I suppose. The mistakes are more important, though."

Which, she thought, said a lot about this man. He was less interested in being rewarded than in correcting his mistakes. She didn't think he'd make many mistakes.

"You have an old soul too," he said abruptly.

Shannon was startled by the comment, and her laugh held no humor. "Then I must have made somebody important in my last life very angry," she managed lightly.

"That cracked mirror," he murmured.

She looked away, disturbed. She trusted that he had told her the truth when he said she was beautiful, but that was only his opinion, after all. Everyone was entitled to his own opinion, no matter how bizarre. And there was her flaw, something she never forgot. No matter what he said about that, she knew the limp existed.

"Shannon—"

The phone rang, cutting off whatever he'd been about to say, and she could only be relieved by that. She felt unsettled, confused. She half listened to his end of the conversation, concentrating on stifling the unusual tangle of emotions she was feeling. And it *was* unusual for her, because she had long ago found a relatively stable position, an even keel for her emotions. If she never allowed her emotions to overwhelm her, she had reasoned, then nothing could hurt too much.

But the past twenty-four hours had held too many emotions for her defenses to stand against. Though she felt physically safe with Derek, there was, on the periphery of awareness, the frightening, numbing sensation of being hunted, like an animal. There was the sense of loss after the destruction of what had been her home. There was the terrifying realization that this virtual stranger beside her was her only lifeline in a treacherous storm. And there was the confusion she felt because he said her mirror was cracked, the reflection she had looked at for so long a distorted one.

Shannon wanted, needed, a moment in which to sit back and catch her breath. A quiet moment in a safe corner somewhere. A moment free of handsome men with ancient eyes, and faceless men who wanted her dead, and a corporation that seemed to be doing something illegal. She needed the safe haven of her drab apartment, as comfortable as a worn shoe and as unthreatening. She needed the secure routine of her ordered life, uninteresting though it was. She needed to get another African violet, because the one in her apartment was dead now. . . .

"Shannon?"

Stupid, she thought, to feel like crying for an African violet. "Was that one of your technician friends?" She looked steadily at her laced fingers.

"Yes. Shannon, what's wrong?"

She could feel him lean closer, and stiffened without even thinking about it. Too close. He was too close. The room was getting small again, closing itself up, filling itself with him, and she could barely breathe. Her throat hurt. "Nothing. What did your friend say?"

Derek moved again, but he was leaning back away from her this time. And his voice was calm and impersonal when he answered her unsteady question. "He said there was some talk a while back about Civatech's 'billion-dollar bust.' They'd apparently gotten military funding for the project, and then reportedly couldn't make the design work."

"What kind of design?" She continued to gaze steadily at her fingers.

"Some kind of sophisticated robotics gadget. Word has it the design was supposed to be practically indestructible, and completely lethal. There was even a rumor circulating at one point that a technician had been killed because the thing ran amok. It seems they couldn't control it, so the design was scrapped. Supposedly."

"And the military just wrote off the loss?" The question was an automatic one, just words to fill a silence.

"Probably. It wouldn't be the first time. But we have to assume that thing is still in one piece, and that somebody's planning either to use it or sell it." He reflected for a moment, frowning. "Probably sell it; it makes more sense. And any fanatical group or army in the world would just love a weapon like that. For a great deterrent, if nothing else. It's a little unsettling to go into battle if you know the other fellow's got a bigger gun."

Derek studied her averted face for a moment, aware that she was tense, guarded. *"Like watching a flower close up."* He had reached her, briefly, and that tenuous thread of trust, he was convinced, remained intact. But it was such a fragile thing, that bond, as fragile as she was herself. Even his leaning toward her in an undemanding physical closeness had tautened it, made her warily conscious of a threatened intrusion.

He kept his voice dispassionate, calm. "We'll have to find out exactly what this design is, and who's planning to use it or sell it. Jeff said they called it Cyrano—" He broke off abruptly, because Shannon looked at him then.

"No," she said in a surprised voice, her eyes widening. "Not Cyrano. C.y.R.A.n.O.W. Camouflage Robotics Armory Offensive Weapon."

After a moment, Derek asked her quietly, "How do you know that, Shannon?"

"I saw it." She shook her head slightly. "I never thought—but that was what was written on it. When I came back from my supervisor's office yesterday, I saw it moving down a hallway. I stopped and watched it. There are all kinds of electronic devices in the building, and I never thought it might be somebody's restricted project. It was in the unrestricted part of the building. But this one was almost funny. Like the gadgets in those science-fiction movies. It was about as high as my shoulder, and had armlike extensions, and it rolled on concealed wheels or something."

"What happened then? Did it just go past you?"

"No. No, a man came hurrying down the hall before it quite reached me. He had a little box in his hand, a remote control, I guess, and he looked angry and—and almost frightened. Shaken. He gave me a hard look, and I turned away and went back to my office."

"And never gave it another thought." Derek sighed heavily. "That was it, I'll bet. If you had just noticed a few oddities and discrepancies, in correspondence, they could have explained it away somehow. But you *saw* their 'scrapped' design alive and well. And they couldn't explain that."

"You mean, just because I saw—"

"It has to be that, Shannon. It was bothering me that they moved so fast and ruthlessly to get you out of the way with apparently so little reason. But if you accidentally saw their gadget on top of everything else, they couldn't take any chances. They couldn't afford to wait, to see if you managed to connect everything."

The phone rang, and Derek half turned to scoop it up quickly from the end table. "Yeah?"

Shannon, watching him, still bewildered, heard the scratching of a shrill voice from the telephone, unintelligible to her. But she listened to Derek's end of the conversation, looking at his face and feeling the tendrils of those unfamiliar emotions fluttering inside her. What was wrong with her? Why did she feel so . . . so restless? So unlike herself.

"Johnny? All right, if the information's worth fifty, I'll leave it in the usual place. What is it?" He listened for a few moments in silence, his face going still. And his voice was flat when he said, "Are you sure? All right. Yeah. I'll leave the money for you. Thanks, Johnny." He cradled the receiver slowly, looked at Shannon for a long moment in silence, then sighed softly.

"Well. It's started."

She felt cold suddenly, something in the flat timbre of his voice alerting her. "What?"

"That was a friend. On the streets. He has good ears, and he just heard there were some unfriendly out-of-towners fresh off a plane trying to find out if I'm in Richmond, or still out of the country. They're also asking about a lovely brunette and flashing a picture of you around."

"A picture? Of me? But, how—"

"You had to get security identification at Civatech, right? An identification with photo?"

Shannon nodded, then frowned. "Unfriendly out-of-towners? What does that mean?" She was afraid she knew.

Derek answered gently, as if he would have softened the blow if he could have. As if anyone could have. "Hit men, Shannon. Assassins."

"But I didn't *do* anything!" she cried.

"That doesn't matter with people like these," Derek told her steadily. "You *could* do something. It's all they know—and it's enough. More than enough. It's a threat to them, and one they have to take care of."

She drew a shuddering breath. "This isn't happening."

"I wish it weren't. But it is. Get your things together, Shannon; we have to leave now. Pack your clothes in that bag I showed you in the bedroom."

His steady voice calmed the panic she felt, and she rose slowly to her feet. He was on his feet as well, facing her, and she looked at him in unconscious pleading, forgetting everything except the terrible need for a sense of stability in a world that had gone mad without warning.

He reached out to touch her shoulders lightly. "I won't let anything happen to you, Shannon."

She tried a smile that didn't quite come off. "Promise?"

"I promise." He smiled. "Now, go pack."

Derek stood where he was until she disappeared into the bedroom, then raked his fingers through his hair as he headed for the hall closet and the bag he kept packed for emergency exits such as this one. Promises. Like a damned bloody fool, he kept making promises, driven to ease the fear in her eyes. And no one knew better than he that promises made in a situation like this were just words written on the wind.

• • •

Derek carried her bag and his own down the service stairs of the building and through a maintenance door he unlocked with a key. He guided her to a dimly lighted parking lot just down the street, stopping only once, briefly, to jam a fifty-dollar bill underneath a pot containing a drooping coleus that was trying rather pathetically and vainly to decorate a low brick wall lining the sidewalk.

He moved quickly, but not so quickly that the pace was too difficult for her to maintain. An unassuming, rather battered Ford was parked nearby, and he unlocked the passenger door and helped Shannon inside. Within minutes of leaving the apartment, they were driving down brightly lighted streets.

It was nearly midnight when a small, dark woman joined a tall companion in the sheltering darkness of an alley between two quiet buildings in a renovated business district. "You have good instincts," she said grudgingly. "How did you know he'd move tonight?"

The tall, athletic man with the colorless eyes continued to stare across the street at an old warehouse recently given a much-needed face-lift and converted to spacious lofts. "Know? I didn't know. How could I? But the pawns in this game seem to be moving with unusual speed. He should have been able to count on another day at least before being forced to abandon the apartment. Interesting."

"You're sure he left because they were too close?"

"He wouldn't have moved otherwise. The girl is—too fragile, I think, to move needlessly."

"And he'd care about that, of course."

The tall man looked down at his companion, his flicker of amusement lost easily in the darkness. "Jealous, Gina?" he asked gently.

She stiffened. "Don't be ridiculous! I'm merely concerned that his emotions not . . . not cloud his judgement. There's too much at stake for such things."

Her companion nodded gravely, the darkness still hiding his expression. "I see. An admirable caution."

She fumed in silence.

He chuckled softly, and changed the subject. "If we are very, very lucky, he saw no sign that he was followed here."

"It's almost impossible to spot a tail if two different cars share the duty," she pointed out in a sharp voice, still obviously annoyed. "And traffic was certainly heavy tonight. He didn't see us, Alexi."

"Perhaps." Softly, as if to himself, Alexi added, "But I have learned never to underestimate his skill—or his instincts. He's been hunter and hunted far too often not to have learned well the tricks of the chase."

Gina looked up at him, frowning slightly. "Sometimes I think you actually like him. Certainly you admire him."

"Is that what you think?" Alexi murmured, and then added, "I'll take the first watch. Relieve me at dawn."

She hesitated, but turned away. And she was making herself as comfortable as possible in her car, parked around the corner, when it occurred to her that Alexi hadn't really answered her implied question about Derek Ross.

Not really.

The loft was huge, open, and airy. It was bi-level, with a raised platform supporting a large, old brass bed, a polished antique mahogany wardrobe, and an equally old rolltop desk; a bathroom and walk-in closet had been built into the upper space in one corner, and a lively schefflera spread its umbrellalike leaves to provide greenery in another corner.

The lower level held a compact kitchen partitioned from the living area by a waist-high counter, and the remainder of the room was casually furnished with a long, overstuffed couch, two comfortable chairs, a wooden rocking chair with a hassock in front of it, end tables, and a coffee table. There were bright rugs on the polished wood floor, the kitchen was stocked with food, and the bed was made up. The place had a lived-in air, but a curious waiting air as well, as if it weren't occupied on a daily basis.

Shannon, sitting in the rocking chair and keeping it moving slowly, watched as Derek made hot cocoa in the kitchen. "Who does this place belong to?"

He looked across the counter at her, taking in her methodical rocking, which obviously hadn't relaxed her. She had been silent all the way here, withdrawn. He couldn't really blame her for that, but he knew how dangerous it was for her to retreat into herself rather than face what was happening. He had to reach her, had to strengthen that tenuous bond between them.

"It belongs to me," he said finally. "But it isn't in my name, and it would take weeks to trace the deed back to me. We're safe here for a while."

She was looking at him, but her eyes were focused on something else, something locked away somewhere inside her. "We moved a lot while I was growing up," she said softly. "Packing and unpacking, a different house or apartment to get used to. Different school. People I didn't know around me. I could never have a pet. And I always felt I—I wasn't a *part* of anything. That I didn't belong anywhere."

Derek hardly realized he was moving toward her; he knew only that the desolate, lost sound of her voice pulled at him like a magnet. He found himself sitting on the hassock and holding both her hands even when she would have instinctively pulled away. Even when she stiffened. His forearms rested just above her knees, and he could feel her tremble.

"Shannon, honey, I know this is hard for you. It would be difficult for someone a hell of a lot tougher and harder than you could ever be. I know you feel lost, confused, scared; you'd have to be made of stone not to. But you *aren't alone*. Do you understand that? I'm with you. I won't leave you, no matter what. And I won't let anyone hurt you."

She looked down at her hands, lost in his, and the sensation of things whirling out of her control gradually slowed, steadied. She felt less dizzy, less cold. Less alone. She shook her head. "I'm sorry, Derek. You're being so kind and I'm falling apart like an idiot—"

"Not like an idiot," he interrupted to correct her. "Like a normal human being, Shannon. You've had one hell of a rug yanked out from under you, and it's only natural to be disoriented and scared. Especially when we had to leave the apartment so suddenly, and you know we may have to move quickly again." His voice altered suddenly, became light and rather pained. "And would you please stop telling me how kind I am? You're going to give me a complex." He squeezed her hands gently, then rose and returned to the kitchen to get the cocoa.

Shannon discovered she was smiling. Had he really called her honey? No. No, of course not. Her imagination. "A complex? It was a compliment."

"Was it?" he asked, carrying two cups from the kitchen and handing her one before sitting at one end of the long couch. "And if I called you a 'dependable sort,' I suppose that would be a compliment?"

She thought about it, and her smile became stronger. "No. No, it wouldn't be."

"Exactly."

After a moment, still smiling, she started rocking again. This time the motion wasn't tensely methodical, but lazy and relaxed. "What happens tomorrow?"

"Tomorrow," he said, "we take it easy. I'll make a couple more phone calls, see if I can find out more about this Cyrano gadget. And we'll go on from there."

Shannon nodded, and he watched her, very conscious of her vulnerability. More relaxed now, she was nonetheless too withdrawn for his peace of mind. Last night, she had been too exhausted and frightened to hide within a shell, too desperate to keep herself from reaching out to someone else for comfort. And now, when she badly needed comfort, needed to be certain she was no longer alone, her wounded self wouldn't allow her to accept reassurance.

He wanted to hold her. But even if she were willing to accept that—and he knew she wasn't—he didn't trust himself. The desire that had coiled in his weary body last night had grown stronger, closer to the surface with every passing hour, and he was fighting to control it. Even assuming she could feel the same for him, such powerful emotions now would very likely send her even deeper into her shell.

Derek had walked many fine lines in his life, performed many a balancing act between safety and danger, but he had never felt such caution within himself as he did now. With Shannon. To say that this situation was the worst possible one in which to begin building a relationship was a vast understatement.

To say that he wanted that relationship more than he had ever wanted anything in his life was a vast understatement.

"I think I'll take a shower," Shannon said, rising to carry her cup into the kitchen.

Derek was too aware of her movements behind him in the kitchen. He watched her climb the stairs and knew she must be taking the silky pajamas Raven had bought her out of the suitcase. He heard her close the bathroom door.

He set his almost-untasted cup of cocoa on the coffee table and frowned at it. He wanted something stronger, but didn't get up to get it. There was, he reflected broodingly, little he could do about the situation at Civatech until he knew more. He'd have to go out there eventually, slip into the place somehow, but he wasn't ready to try that just yet.

Was it less than twenty-four hours ago that Shannon had come into his life? Odd that events had a way of stretching time in improbable ways. Still, it was something he had seen happen more than once. He wasn't sure if he had lived a week's normal time at any point during the past ten years or so. One of these days he'd have to drop back into normal life, with its hectic but predictable schedule, and he'd probably suffer jet lag from the shock to his system.

One of these days.

His mind, never very far from Shannon, focused on her more intently as he heard the shower running. Cautious as he was toward her, he knew only too well that he couldn't allow her to remain withdrawn. He had to reach her somehow. There was, inside that guarded, wounded woman, a vividly alive and laughing woman hidden away. He knew it. He *felt* it.

She was stronger than she knew—she would have had to be to weather the shocks and pain of her life. She was innately a very strong woman; yes, he knew that as surely as he knew his own strengths and weaknesses. But she was so accustomed to being alone inside herself that withdrawal had become a part of her personality rather than a simple defense mechanism. And how could he teach this hurt, guarded woman to allow him close enough to share the careful space she had marked out for her own?

It was what he had tried to do in explaining that she had to trust him. And though that first step had forged a tenuous bond. Shannon refused to let him close the distance between them. She needed time alone, safe time, he knew that. She needed to find a balance, to catch her breath. The problem was, he couldn't give her that.

The only safe time he could give her would be fleeting and uncertain, with the probability of fast action and danger hovering over them like a sword.

Derek knew rationally that he was in no shape for this. It was beyond his experience. He was adept at functioning on little rest under stressful conditions, but he had never before had to do so with a fragile victim depending on him for her very life. And if he had been asked theoretically if he could have done so while also being emotionally involved with that fragile woman, he would have answered with an unequivocal *no*. But the question was hardly a theoretical one.

He was here. She was dependent on him for her safety, her life. And he was emotionally involved with her despite every atom of good sense.

"Derek?"

He looked over at the steps of the platform, where Shannon stood hesitantly. The pajamas she wore provided adequate coverage, since they were long and plainly styled, with a top that was buttoned all the way to her throat. But the cream silk lent the outfit its feminine appearance as it clung like a living thing, and the slender curves of Shannon's body were as seductively obvious to his intent eyes as they would have been clothed only in a brief silk teddy.

Score one for Raven. Derek thought vaguely as

he felt his belly knot in a sudden rush of heat. He'd told her that Shannon had injured a leg and was sensitive, and had asked the other woman not to buy too-revealing clothing that might make Shannon feel uncomfortable. He hadn't said anything about not making *him* uncomfortable, though.

"I can sleep on the couch," Shannon offered a bit breathlessly, disturbed by his steady look and silence. "You couldn't have gotten much rest last night, and—"

"You take the bed." He smiled. "The years have trained me. Like most soldiers, I can sleep anywhere, probably even standing on my head."

"Are you sure?"

"Positive." Derek wondered if he was imagining that he could smell a delicate floral scent wafting to him from her; there was no soap with that scent in the loft. Had Raven taken care of that too? If so, he could blame her for a quick rise in his blood pressure. He cleared his throat strongly and concentrated on keeping his expression neutral. "I'll probably be up for a while. Will the light down here bother you?"

"No." She hesitated another minute, then turned away toward the bed.

Derek got up to turn off the overhead light anyway, leaving only the lamp by the couch on. He was unusually aware of the rustle of bedclothes in the silence, and reminded himself he was a grown man and perfectly capable of controlling his hormones. It didn't help. He hadn't really expected it to.

He went into the kitchen to the hidden control box for his security system: Shannon hadn't noticed and he deliberately hadn't pointed it out to her. The box was concealed behind what looked like just another section of the painted brick wall, opening to his familiar touch by a hidden spring. He set the system with the necessary codes, activating the alarms set at both downstairs doors and all the windows. Another switch activated timers in the three other lofts in the building so that lights would come on and go off at irregular intervals, suggesting the lofts were inhabited, which they weren't.

He set three final switches: One to activate pressure alarms on the roof, one to turn on motion-sensors and cameras placed strategically around the building, and the third switch to alert the building's very dependable caretaker, who lived nearby, that Derek was "in residence" and not to be disturbed.

Shannon didn't know it, but she was sleeping in a virtual fortress.

Having done everything possible to ensure an advance warning for them in case of visitors, Derek moved back toward the couch. It wasn't until he glanced at the bed and saw Shannon sitting up that he realized she had watched his actions.

"Who are you, Derek?" she asked softly.

The light provided by the lamp barely reached her, and she was only an insubstantial shape, her silky pajamas reflecting the light in a faint shimmer. Derek sat on the couch because he didn't dare remain standing; his body was having ideas that his mind found difficult to deny. "You know who I am."

"I wonder if anybody does. William would be surprised if he saw this place, wouldn't he?"

Derek didn't think it likely. "In a fox hunt," he said quietly, "the fox always has more than one way out of his burrow—if he's smart. I've been hunted before, Shannon, so I've taken the idea a step farther. More than one burrow. And always more than one way out of each."

"What's the other way out of this burrow?"

He smiled faintly. "There's a trap door inside the closet, and a tunnel leading to an outbuilding. James Bond stuff," he mocked himself lightly.

Shannon hugged her upraised knees and watched him, not yet ready to sleep because she was afraid she'd dream. "Has it been exciting—your life?"

"I wouldn't have stayed in this business otherwise," he answered. "There are always benefits to my work. I've seen parts of the world the tourists will never see, for instance."

"And the drawbacks?"

Derek fished a package of cigarettes from his pocket and lit one. "Those too."

After a moment of silence, she said, "You don't want to talk about the drawbacks?"

No, he didn't. Not to her. Not now, at least, when she was living under the threat of some of those drawbacks. "You should get some sleep, honey."

Shannon slid down in the bed and drew the covers up, gazing at a shadowy ceiling. He *had* called her honey this time. But it probably didn't mean anything. She wished it did. Wished she could tell him how afraid she was to sleep, because she wasn't too tired to dream tonight. Wished she could ask him to just hold her because—

She felt shaken suddenly. Shocked. When had she ever asked anyone for that kind of physical closeness? It was hardly something she was used to. Her mother wasn't a physically demonstrative woman, and Shannon had always felt stiff and uneasy whenever someone came too close. Why was she longing, now, for strong arms around her and the comforting sound of another heart beating under her ear?

Because she was afraid? Or was it something else, something about Derek? Was that longing for his touch all tangled with her stark awareness of him? Stupid. *Stupid!* She'd been hung around his neck like an albatross, and that was all. The poor man was being forced to cope, no only with threats against him because of her, but with her fears, and—

"Shannon?"

He was standing by the bed, silhouetted by the lamp behind him on the lower level, his very outline unnervingly masculine and heart-catchingly powerful. And her heart jumped into an uneven rhythm as it thudded against her ribs. How had he known? What *was* he that he always seemed to know how she was feeling?

"I'm all right," she said, and they both knew she wasn't.

Four

Derek sat down on the edge of the bed and gently captured one of her hands that was twisting on top of the covers. Her hand was cold and tense in his for a long moment, but gradually relaxed. Quietly, he said, "It's always worse at night, isn't it? The darkness closes in, and it's easy to feel like you're alone. But you aren't, Shannon."

"I'm sorry," she said jerkily. "You're in this mess because of me, and I can't even make it easier for you. I want to be strong, but I can't stop thinking about them out there looking for us as if we were animals being hunted! And I know *I'm* one of those drawbacks you didn't want to talk about, tied around your neck and just weighing you down—"

"Stop it, Shannon." His voice was abruptly sharp. "Do you really think you'd be with me if I didn't want it that way? I could have had you hidden away in a protective custody somewhere until we got this whole thing sorted out. I could have sent you with Raven: the security system set up around her and her husband is one of the best I've ever seen. Hell, I could have called the cops and had *them* take care of you. You're with me because I *want* you with me."

"Just because you feel responsible—"

"No." He hesitated, then said dryly, "Maybe it's my ego saying I can take care of you better than anyone else. Maybe it's those big brown eyes of yours—or the way you looked in that damned red dress." He felt her hand tense again, and wondered if he'd gone too far. How far could he go to get close to her without pushing her even farther away?

"It wasn't even my dress." Her voice was low, shy.

He laughed softly, and purposely kept his voice light and unthreatening. "It was yours once you put it on. A dress like that on a woman like you could make a grown man cry. Or start writing sonnets in his mind. Unfortunately, I have no creative ability when it comes to words, and that dumb macho ethic kept me from breaking into tears."

She laughed shakily. "So what do you do?"

"I bit down on a knuckle when you weren't looking," he told her solemnly.

Shannon laughed again, honestly amused. "I can't see you doing that."

"I don't want you to see me doing that," he said in a reproving tone. "It ruins my tough manly image. I debated whether to cook for you, but decide in the end that since there are so many male gourmets, I was pretty safe."

"You showed talent as a masseur too," she reminded gravely.

"*Masseur.*" He corrected her pronunciation in a grand French accent. "If you know the French for a thing, it takes away any gender connotations."

"I would have thought it was the other way around," she said with a little choke of laughter. "The French seem fairly conscious of gender."

After a deliberate moment, Derek said consideringly, "You could be right there. I may have sacrificed my tough manly image by—no, I forgot, that was in another life. Just some residual technique left over for this life. So I'm safe." Her hand was relaxed now in his, and warm, and her laugh was rich with humor. A part of him was elated, but there was another cautious part that reminded him it was easier to find closeness in the dark than in the light.

"I think you really are a magician," she said suddenly in a surprised tone.

"Well, legerdemain is a nice, masculine talent," he allowed seriously. "I won't object to that."

She chuckled and said, "I feel better now. Thank you, Derek."

He didn't want to leave her, even though it was costing him to remain there. Common sense and caution won out over the demands of his body, and he squeezed her hand briefly before rising to his feet. "Good. Now get a good night's sleep, honey." He was at the steps when she spoke again.

"Derek?"

He paused and looked back at her.

"What did you mean—a woman like me?"

He didn't need the question clarified. "You're beautiful, Shannon," he said quietly. "Some day I'll teach you to believe that."

After a moment, she whispered, "Good night."

"Good night, honey." Derek returned to the lower level and sat down on the couch, trying consciously to relax taut muscles in an effort he knew to be worthless.

How much more easily she responded to him in the darkness! As if darkness were the only wall she needed then, and light brought her self-made walls rising instantly. Only in the darkness had he heard her laugh; only in the darkness had he heard the intriguing note in her voice that was so vividly alive it made his heart stop.

That was the real Shannon, he thought, coming alive in the darkness like some rare and fragile flower that showed its blooms only to the night. Was it because of her leg? Partly, he thought; the core of that characteristic could probably be found in her constant awareness of her flaw. In the darkness she couldn't be seen, and her self-consciousness vanished.

He could reach her then, in the darkness. Closer one step at a time, unthreatening and undemanding. And the cost to him would be well worth the result if he managed to reach her fully. But he didn't deceive himself that it would be easy. No, it wouldn't be easy.

Derek lit a cigarette and broodingly watched his hands tremble. Not easy at all. Grown man or not, he was finding it more and more difficult to control the desire he felt for her. He had never felt anything like this, and the strength of it had caught him off guard. Those big brown eyes—or that dress. Who knew what had done it?

She had come to him out of desperate need for his help and, with the worst timing possible, he had fallen in love.

There was probably, he thought, nothing on earth as fundamentally impatient as a man in love. It was entirely natural at such a mad turning point in one's life to be intolerant of any delay, to be wholly resistant to the idea of cautious equanimity, and to be possessed by a primitive physical desire that had to be beaten into some semblance of submission. Or satisfied.

Entirely natural.

And to force patience at such a moment went totally against the nature of the beast. So much so, at least in his own case, that Derek wasn't sure he could do it. Love made desire more than itself, made it a hungry need just barely under control. But for how long?

Could he manage to control his own need long enough to reach Shannon and build that vital trust? And, even then . . . could he get close enough to touch her heart?

Raven hung up the phone and leaned back against the desk in their suite. "Damn," she said softly.

Josh, standing a few feet away and gazing out a window at a sunny morning, turned toward her. "I didn't like the sound of your end of the conversation," he noted. "Bad?"

"It isn't good. You remember I asked a friend of mine in the police department here to let me know if anything happened near Derek's apartment?"

"I remember." Josh came to her, his rather hard blue eyes softening as always when they rested on his wife. "What's happened?"

"The alarm Derek had rigged in his apartment woke the neighborhood around two this morning.

Witnesses reported two men running from the building. When the police got there, they found the door forced and the place empty. No sign of violence other than the door; they were looking for people, not things."

Josh frowned. "Two men. Then Derek wasn't there when they broke in."

Raven sighed. "He always has pretty good street connections wherever he is. And he told me he expected them to find him just because he was a *possible* danger. If he was warned in time, then he's taken Shannon and gone to ground somewhere."

"Any ideas where?"

Her smile was crooked. "I think I told you once that all of us secret agent types had a speciality? Well, Derek's is the ability to disappear—thoroughly. I told him we'd help if he needed a safe house, but I'm willing to bet he has half a dozen of his own scattered around Richmond . . . just in case."

Josh looked at her for a moment, then asked politely, "Just who *is* Derek?"

She grinned. "You caught that, huh?"

"A number of safe houses," Josh said, "even if only broom closets, tend to run into money. How does he manage on a government salary?"

"He doesn't," she replied, smiling. "A few years ago, I found out quite by accident who Derek is—and why Hagen never ordered him around like the rest of us peons."

"I was wondering about that too," Josh confessed.

"It's crystal clear once you know the facts. Derek, the black sheep of his family, is also the heir. And you being a man of business surely know the Ross-Garrett Corporation?"

After a moment, Josh grimaced faintly. "What was that he said to me during that little caper with Kelsey about it being nice to have clout? He should know, dammit."

"Understated, that's Derek."

Reflectively, Josh said, "I'm glad now that I decided against a takeover bid of Ross-Garrett. I have a feeling it wouldn't be smart to back Derek into a corner."

"Not if you value your throat," Raven murmured.

"He goes straight for the jugular, eh?" Josh looked at her with a gleam in his eyes. "Who would you put money on, darling?"

She returned the look with a faint smile. "Don't bite me, but when it comes to Ross-Garrett, I'd back Derek. His grandfather built that company, and even though Derek doesn't have much to do with the running of it, he'd die a bloody death before giving it up to anyone."

Josh whistled softly. "Like that, is it? Then I'd say a man with those kinds of instincts can take care of himself."

"I know." She sighed again. "And he can take care of Shannon. But he's involved this time, and it's a first for him."

"Happened fast," Josh noted.

"You should understand that, darling."

He grinned at her. "I seem to recall." He leaned over to kiss her, and then straightened and looked back over his shoulder as Zach came into the living room of the suite.

"Am I interrupting again?" the big security chief asked.

Raven leaned sideways to peer around Josh. "No more than usual," she told him gently. "We're getting used to it."

Zach smiled at her, then reached over the back of the couch for a set of rolled-up blueprints. "The engineer on that Kansas City job is confused about the security system," he told his friend and employer. "I've got him on the phone. Are you two going out for lunch?"

Josh glanced at his wife, then said, "No. Room service."

Zach relaxed almost imperceptibly. He half saluted them with the blueprints, then vanished into his own room.

"He still doesn't look like himself," Raven said softly.

"He took it as hard as Teddy did," Josh agreed quietly. "And losing the baby was bad enough—almost losing Teddy scared the hell out of him." He frowned. "I wish he'd stayed with her in Boston. I know she's recovered now and wanted him here with us while she's resting at her sister's place, but—"

"But," Raven finished gently, "the threats against you are a more deadly danger at the moment. If Teddy had needed Zach, nothing could have kept him from her, you know that."

Josh agreed with a reluctant nod. "I know. But threats are fairly common, and with Zach's security team around us, a gnat couldn't get in here, much less an armed gnat."

Raven slipped her arms around his waist. "Well, we'll be heading back to New York in a few days. In the meantime, if Derek *does* ask for our help—?"

"Then we give it," Josh said promptly. "If he hadn't acted so quickly in England, I would've had to fall flat at your feet in Red Square."

"The logistics would have been tricky," she agreed with a solemn nod.

He kissed her. "Indeed. And, speaking of logistics, is there anything along those lines we can do for Derek?"

Raven looked innocent. "He said he didn't want us getting involved. Said it rather fiercely, as a matter of fact."

Josh eyed her. "Oh, he did, did he? Just because I don't want to take over the man's company doesn't mean I'm going to let him push me around."

"I thought you might say something like that, darling," she murmured, smiling.

Derek didn't give Shannon a chance to withdraw completely from him that day, though she would have. He gritted his teeth and managed to control his unruly impulses, concentrating on closing the distance between them as unthreateningly as possible. Considered by others a nerveless man, he was fast discovering that his supposedly nonexistent nerves could come alive because she smiled at him, and that his heart had developed a disconcerting habit of stopping suddenly whenever he touched her.

And he touched her often. Sharing the duties of cooking breakfast in the small kitchen provided opportunities, and he didn't hesitate to take advantage of them, whether it was a guiding touch on her shoulder or a firm hand around hers to demonstrate the proper way to flip a pancake. He forced himself to be as casual as possible, matter-of-fact, but he was also firm and quite deliberate. He was still gauging her reactions very carefully, trying to move slowly.

It hadn't taken very long at all for him to realize

that there was no lover waiting somewhere in the background; a large part of Shannon's reaction to his touch was sheer surprise. The light, flirtatious conversation of the night before, conducted in darkness, had not prepared her even to consider that Derek's casual touches meant a very personal interest.

And even though he'd intended to keep everything on an impersonal basis as long as possible in order to gain her trust, that restless male part of him that loved and wanted began to get the upper hand. It wasn't a conscious decision that his touches began to linger and his voice drop to a new lower note, and he wasn't even aware of it until he saw her increased surprise and wary confusion.

And by then he wasn't sure he could stop it.

A distraction presented itself when Derek made a few calls, checking out Civatech with one friend and asking another to find out what he could about the company's director of design, Adam Moreton. Shannon was restless while he made those calls, wandering around the loft as if she couldn't settle in one place. Derek watched her, wondering if the restlessness was because the calls had reminded her of the danger again, or if his own behavior had unsettled her.

She was limping.

"Anything?" she asked when he cradled the receiver at last.

"We may know something later today," he told her.

"Can they find us here? Those men?"

Derek hesitated, then answered truthfully, "Anyone can be found with enough time. But it'll be damned hard for them to find us here. Shannon, is your leg bothering you?"

She immediately stopped moving, sitting down on the second step leading up to the platform. "It isn't hurting."

She had stopped, he thought wryly, with almost the length of the room between them. Hardly a good sign. "That isn't what I asked."

Shannon seemed to become fascinated by the tight cuff of her gold silk blouse, pulling at a button methodically. "It isn't bothering me," she murmured.

"Then why were you limping?" He lit a cigarette, more to keep his hands busy than anything else.

After a moment, she said tightly, "I limp. I can't help it."

"You only limp when your leg hurts and when you start thinking about it. You said it didn't hurt. So why were you thinking about it just now?"

"I wasn't."

"You were limping."

Shannon pulled harder at the button.

He sighed softly. "It must be those big brown eyes. You're getting to me now, and there's no sign of a red dress."

She shot him a quick, startled look. "You don't have to say things like that."

"I thought so," he said quietly, watching her. "Not only don't you believe me when I say you're beautiful, but you honestly have no idea how much you really *are* getting to me. Are you afraid of it, Shannon, or do you just not believe it?"

"I don't know what you're talking about," she

said unsteadily, bewildered by him and by the turmoil of feelings inside her. She wanted to touch him, wanted to laugh or cry, or do something insanely reckless. . . .

Derek leaned forward to stub out his cigarette in an ashtray on the coffee table, paying strict attention to the task. "God knows I don't want to scare you," he said in a low voice. "You've been scared enough. And hurt enough. But I want you to understand—and believe—that you are a lovely, desirable woman, and that I want you very much."

Shannon couldn't breathe, but didn't think it mattered. Her heart wasn't beating either, and then it was pounding erratically. He was several feet away in a large room, but she thought she could reach out and touch him. She could see individual golden hairs on his forearm and the curious flecks of color in his dark eyes. She could see the faint white line of tension around his mouth, and the tautness in his jaw. He was sitting back on the couch, turning his head to look at her, and his smile was lopsided, almost casual.

But there was that tension around his mouth. And had there been a faint tremor in that beautiful deep voice of his?"

"No," she said huskily, unable to look away. "Men don't want me."

"I can't speak for all men," he said quietly. "But I'd hate to think so many were morons. This man wants you, Shannon. I don't want to take advantage of what's happening in your life right now, but you had to know. I couldn't have hidden it much longer. You could see that, couldn't you? It's why you were limping. Because I couldn't hide what I was feeling, and you couldn't believe it.

Damn that distorted mirror," he added without heat.

He was right: She couldn't believe it. Men didn't want her. And for a man like Derek to say that he did . . . no, she couldn't believe it.

"I could prove it to you," he said, still without moving from the couch. "But if I started loving you, I'd never be able to stop." He wanted to tell her that "loving" was a literal term, but knew she wouldn't believe that either. "And you'd believe it was just an appetite I wanted to satisfy, that it didn't matter which woman was in my bed. You'd hurt yourself for no reason, and that would hurt me." He drew a deep breath. "Which is why I'm sitting here hurting in other ways while trying to convince myself that I'm a grown man and I can't always have what I want."

Shannon cleared her throat carefully, and wasn't surprised when her voice emerged shakily. "You seem to have me pretty well figured out."

"I wish that were true."

"It's just—propinquity."

"No," he said, as if he'd expected just that argument from her.

"It doesn't make sense," she whispered.

He smiled another crooked smile. "It's the only thing that does. The situation is impossible, the timing is lousy, and I want you." Evenly, he added, "I shouldn't have to say this, but after what you've gone through it's only natural for you to look at this situation with suspicion. So I'll say it. Trite as it sounds, I don't mix business and pleasure, Shannon; in *my* business, it's stupid, and it's dangerous. This is a first for me. Also, I have never in my life believed that any woman should pay off a real or imagined debt to me in bed."

Shannon looked hastily back at her sleeve and plucked at the button again, feeling heat suffuse her face. The man was a magician, a warlock. He always knew—

"That is what you were thinking, isn't it?" he asked gently.

After a moment, she said huskily, "It was the only thing that made sense."

"You don't have a very high opinion of yourself, but we knew that. Now we know you don't think much of me either."

"That isn't fair," she whispered.

"Probably not." His voice was suddenly clipped, remote. "I'm finding it a little difficult to look at the situation objectively. I know you're hurt, Shannon. I know you've been hurt a long time. What your life's done to you makes me mad as hell— and not only because of what it's done to *you*, but also because of what it's going to do to us."

She cleared her throat. "What do you mean?"

Derek sighed. And his voice lost the hard remoteness, deepening and going rough when he answered. "You're as wary as a little stray cat, afraid to be touched, suspicious of every outstretched hand. Too proud to reach out yourself, far too certain you'll receive a slap instead of a welcome. You were like that before this whole thing started. And now it's worse. You've lost your home, you're being hunted by deadly people. And I'm a stranger. If you were afraid to trust before, you're a hundred times less likely to trust now. Especially a stranger. Especially a man who says he wants you."

"I said I—I trusted you."

"You trust me to know best how to handle the

situation with Civatech. You trust me to know when to run, and where to run. But you don't trust me as a man, Shannon. And I'm afraid we aren't going to have very much time to build that bridge. I'm afraid, too, because I want you so much. And, because we're in the situation we're in, more or less trapped together, I'm afraid I'll rush you, overwhelm you. You're confused and scared, and God knows I don't want to take advantage."

Shannon drew a deep breath. "So what are you saying?"

Derek reached for a cigarette, lit it. He wasn't looking at her now, and his voice was still rough. "I'm saying there's no easy solution. I'm not going to stop wanting you, no matter how many times I tell myself I can't have what I want. But I'll try to control it. And the situation with Civatech will likely get much worse before it gets better, until it's over for good. Time won't stand still for us; there'll always be that threat. Until it's over."

She hesitated. "You're saying you want me, but we won't—won't—"

"Make love." He made the words evenly spaced and distinct. "That's what I'm saying. The timing is lousy, and I won't do anything to add more fear and confusion to your life. When all this is over, when your life is stable again and you can think clearly, then we'll see how you feel about it. You could decide I'm the last man in the world you'd be attracted to. But I want you to make the decision. I don't want you to feel rushed—by me or by the circumstances."

He looked at her then, his expression serious and his dark eyes intent. "Do you understand,

Shannon? I can't help wanting you; but whether or not you really want me is a decision you won't have to make until you have the time and peace to think it through." Promises, he thought, and wondered if he could keep this one. Wondered if he'd sacrifice his sanity to keep this one. "All right?"

After a moment, she nodded hesitantly. "All right."

"Just don't be afraid of me." He hoped his smile didn't look as strained as it felt. "And don't be afraid of what I feel for you."

Shannon's nod was more hesitant this time, almost a cross between a nod and a head-shake, reflecting her confusion. Her gaze skittered away from his. She didn't know what she felt, but if there was fear it was lost in the turmoil of a dozen other emotions. Her throat was tight and scratchy, and her heart beat with a slow, heavy rhythm, as if some internal pressure delayed every beat. Her skin felt flushed, tingling as if her nerve endings were closer to the surface now.

Something inside her was shaking, trembling. She couldn't believe he really wanted her. Not *her*. He'd probably been breaking hearts since his teens with that smile, his dark eyes, and he'd break hers if she let him . . . or even if she didn't. Let. Such a simple word. There wouldn't, she thought, be any *let* about it. Just as there wouldn't be any peaceful, logical decision for her no matter what happened.

Didn't he know that? Did he know she was already overwhelmed, afraid of how he made her feel? Afraid of him . . . . If she could have run from him now, she would have. When all this was over, she'd run. A man like Derek wouldn't be interested in her anymore once her particular crisis was over, and she wouldn't wait for him to tell her that. She wouldn't wait to be hurt.

You're a coward, Shannon! Cowardly Shannon, always running because it hurt too much to stay. Running from her mother. From the failures of lost jobs and the wounds of pitying looks. Scurrying from one boring but safe shelter to another, one drab apartment to another. Walking carefully, speaking softly. Afraid to risk anything of herself. And now, when a man showed interest in her, she'd run again.

The man was ordinary. He was average in height, build, coloring. His clothing was unobtrusive, his stride even and steady. He didn't turn his head left or right as he walked, but a perceptive observer would have noted that his muddy brown eyes moved ceaselessly back and forth, back and forth, scanning his surroundings with the automatic intensity of old habit.

There were several phone booths, the old-fashioned enclosed kind, near a corner of the busy street, and he entered one with the faint frown of a man with things on his mind. He didn't have to fumble for change since it was already in his hand, and he quickly deposited it and punched out the number he wanted. After a few seconds, there were several clicks and buzzes on the line, and he waited with outward patience.

"Yes." The voice was guarded, muffled, completely unidentifiable.

"They were gone." The man's eyes continued to scan his surroundings, and his own voice was cool and matter-of-fact. "An alarm system, of course."

After a moment of silence, the voice hissed, "You should have had them. A bomb, or—"

"You've blown up one building without success," the man interrupted curtly. "My partner and I don't work that way; you knew it when you hired us."

"All right, all right." There was anger in the voice, almost rage, followed by the sounds of several deep breaths being drawn.

The man waited patiently, his lips twisting in a grimace. Childish games, he thought. The line had been scrambled at the other end; he recognized that peculiarly hollow quality to the connection. As if he didn't know who it was he worked for on this job. They thought it protected them, the faceless, nameless men who tended to seek his services. They thought that they were beyond his reach, should something go wrong.

He laughed about that sometimes.

"All right," the voice repeated, calm now. "I'll find out where they've gone to ground."

"He's an experienced agent, by all accounts," the man said dryly. "It won't be easy."

"I'll find out. Call me back around midnight." There was an abrupt click, and then the dial tone.

The man left the phone booth and walked away, still casual. And he wondered idly what it felt like to have the kind of power his employer demonstrated.

Tension built in Shannon as the day wore on. Derek was casual, keeping the conversation on theoretical possibilities about who could be involved at Civatech. He had her close her eyes and describe the layouts of the parts of the building she'd seen, while he sketched a diagram. He questioned her about the security system, inside and out. About procedures.

Shannon might have forgotten or doubted that the earlier tense conversation had taken place, except that Derek gave himself away. Whenever she was near, he couldn't seem to prevent himself from touching her, sometimes drawing his hand away hastily after a fleeting contact. His voice roughened from time to time, and he'd quickly clear his throat and go on as if nothing had happened. He watched her all the time, even when he was on the phone trying to gather information about Civatech and get a "line" on the men hunting them.

His obvious awareness heightened her own, making it impossible for her to completely withdraw from him. She was too conscious of him to hide herself away, too confused by her own feelings to rebuild the wall his stark admission of desire had sent tumbling down. She caught herself limping a few times, knowing he saw it, too, and gradually accepted that he'd been right about that, at least. Conscious of him, she was more conscious of herself, more aware of her imperfect body.

As night came, her own restless tension became something she could barely control. She prepared the evening meal while Derek talked on the phone with another friend, this one having heard a bit more about Civatech or "Cyrano." Derek had explained that he wanted to safely gather as much information as possible today before making the difficult decision of what to do about the matter.

And the knowledge that something *had* to be done, that it wouldn't end by itself, just added to

Shannon's strain. As always in her life, things were happening beyond her control, and the sense of helplessness was demoralizing. All she could do was wait and be prepared to run. The worst of it was that she sensed Derek was more inclined to turn and fight instantly despite the advance preparation of his "burrows." Instead, he had chosen this hide-and-seek game, and that told her only too clearly and painfully that she was a handicap, that he had to consider her protection in all his future plans.

She felt a growing scorn for herself along with the restlessness, a gnawing sense of being powerless when she should have been able to *do* something. She couldn't even be a normally strong woman; instead, she cringed like a frightened child. Oh, she knew rationally that being hunted like an animal would test the courage of anyone. But what about the other? Did every woman start falling to pieces because a man said he wanted her? No. And why had she? Because she was *afraid*.

She was tired of being afraid.

Derek offered to clean up after the meal, and Shannon slipped away to take a bath, hoping the hot water would warm her cold hands and ease the tension. But it didn't. The huge, old clawfooted tub, likely claimed from some junkyard by an ambitious decorator and restored to its former pristine whiteness, was almost deep enough for her to swim in, but not even her vague amusement at it relieved the tension she felt.

She dried off and dressed in the silk pajamas — even though it was still fairly early. She had realized that the finely honed look of Derek's handsome face spoke of too little rest, and thought if she went to bed early he might rest tonight. That was why he was so tense and restless himself, she decided firmly. He was just more tired than usual, and despite what he'd said about mixing business and pleasure, she couldn't believe a man with all his undeniable attractions was accustomed to spending even a few days without some woman happily in his bed—

Shannon felt a stab of pain so sharp then that she caught her breath and braced one hand on the sink, staring at her white face in the mirror. Automatically, she rubbed her hip with her free hand, even though she knew the pain hadn't come from that old injury. Her mind went blank, walled-off, refusing even to consider the possibility. She waited until that face in the mirror had lost its look of shock, until the eyes were calm again. Then she left the bathroom.

Five

She was serene, tranquil. Outwardly and inwardly. The utter stillness inside her seemed a good thing to her, a welcome thing, and Shannon had no way of knowing it was like the hushed silence before an earthquake. She had no way of knowing, unaccustomed as she was to emotional highs and lows, that her kind of composure was a terribly fragile layer of calm over emotions that were seething.

And the shock, when it came, was so sudden that she could only respond with equal suddenness, completely out of instinct. She was standing on the bottom step going down into the softly lighted living area, looking at Derek as he stood to stretch cramped muscles and frowned down at the diagram and notes littering the coffee table.

Shannon opened her mouth to ask some unformed question, and that was when they both heard the sharp, echoing report from outside, chillingly loud and stark in the silence of the night.

Derek turned toward her instantly, but even then he barely had time to realize she had moved before she was in his arms, shaking violently. Her reaction came from nothing rational, but from the primitive fear of loud noises that any hunted animal would have shared.

"Shannon . . ." He held her tightly, aware of nothing in those first seconds but the desire to reassure and comfort her. "It was just a car, honey, backfiring. It's all right." He smoothed her thick hair and murmured wordlessly, but her trembling body wouldn't stop shaking. And when she lifted her face from his chest and looked up at him, he realized that something had changed, something irrevocable. He thought he even knew what it was, and tried to save them both from what was happening by explaining to her.

"Shannon, sometimes a primitive emotion like fear will trigger another one." He heard his voice hoarsening, felt his belly knot hard in a rush of heated desire, and tried to fight his spiraling senses even as his arms unconsciously tightened around her slender, trembling body. "It's natural."

"Is it?" She was staring up at him, her voice slow and wondering, dazed. She thought she'd fallen over the brink of something, was still falling wildly, and for some reason she couldn't do a thing to save herself. "I've never felt this way before."

Derek knew what he should have done. He should have gently released her, pulled her arms from around his waist and stepped away from her. He should have made some light comment and turned both their minds from the unexpected physical encounter, managing somehow not to hurt her needlessly by making her feel rejected.

That was what he should have done.

He knew even as his head lowered toward hers that this was a mistake, and a faint despairing voice in his mind told him he'd pay dearly for it later. But he had to kiss her, the way a starving man has to take sustenance, or a thirsting man has to drink. The demand of his clamoring body wouldn't be denied. His need for her was as primitive as the need for security she had shown when she'd instinctively leapt into his arms.

At the first touch of her cool, trembling lips, what might have been a tentative first kiss, what should have been just that, exploded between them violently with a force that jarred them both. Shannon stiffened for an instant, almost crying out, and then her arms tightened fiercely around his lean waist and her fingers dug into the rippling muscles of his back as she melted completely, bonelessly against him. The detonation of that kiss shocked everything inside her, senses and emotions and rationality, leaving behind nothing but burning need.

Dizziness flowed over her and a faint sound tangled in the back of her throat when his mouth slanted over hers, deepening the devastating kiss with a surge of possession that rocked her to her soul. The duel of tongues was shocking in its molten heat, vibrantly exciting in its mutual need and searing intimacy. She was vividly aware that her body was changing as it pressed against his, that her breasts were swelling and aching, her limbs weakening, her veins running with fire. It was a combination of feelings so intensely alive that she wouldn't have fought them no matter what.

She barely heard Derek groan, but felt the vibration of the sound. She felt one of his hands slide down her silk-clad back to her hips, pressing her even closer to his hardening body, and a shudder of raw desire went through her at the starkly intimate sensation.

He ended the kiss suddenly, tearing his mouth from hers with an effort that was almost violent. "Shannon . . . you don't know what you're doing," he said hoarsely, unable to resist the soft flesh of her throat.

"Yes, I do." She could feel his other hand at the back of her head, his fingers moving in her hair caressingly, and lifted her chin to allow him more room to explore as his lips trailed down her throat. Eyes half-closed, she was mindlessly basking in the radiant fire of his body and her own. It was so warm. *He* was so warm and hard, and she needed him so badly. She couldn't catch her breath and didn't care; didn't care about anything but these wonderful feelings.

"Stop me," he whispered tensely against her throat. "For your sake—stop me!"

"Not even for my sake," she murmured, wondering why he would say something like that. Why on earth would she want to stop him? She felt so alive, so wonderfully alive, and so much a woman. For the first time in her adult life, she truly felt like a woman. And she could feel the strength inside herself for the first time, a tempered steel core that had lain hidden beneath fears this explosion had ripped away: it was a strength she hadn't imagined herself capable of, and she gloried in the knowledge that it existed within her.

Wonderingly, she repeated, "Not even for my sake. Make love to me, Derek." And there was no shock left in the astonishing freedom she felt in that moment.

Even then, Derek might have been able to stop himself, because he knew what he stood to lose in the recklessness of his need and her response. And if Shannon had shown one instant's hesitation, one flicker of uncertainty, it would have been enough to give him the strength he needed. But more than her words told him she wouldn't hesitate. Her body told him. She was moving restlessly against him, unconsciously seeking, and her trembling hands stroked his back, tried to draw him closer. And he couldn't fight them both.

He tried. *Dear God, he tried!* His head lifted, his body stiffening with the fierce effort to take that first step back away from her. But Shannon's arms slipped from around his waist and her hands fumbled with the buttons of his shirt, and when he felt her seeking touch, felt her lips as she pressed them to his chest, he knew he wouldn't be able to do it.

"Shannon . . ." It was little more than a breath of sound. He framed her face in his hands and kissed her with all the gentle restraint he could manage, making a silent promise to her and to himself that this wouldn't be a mistake. That he wouldn't let this be a mistake. Then he lifted her into his arms and carried her up the steps and to the side of the bed.

She felt right in his arms, just as she had that

first night, and he was reluctant to let her go enough to set her on her feet by the bed. He couldn't stop touching her, couldn't stop gazing into the dark amber fire of her eyes. She was so beautiful it almost stopped his heart.

Shannon was hardly aware they'd moved. She was vaguely conscious of the bed behind her, but could only gaze up at his taut, handsome face and marvel at her own feelings. These strange new feelings that had brought her alive. "I want you," she said wonderingly.

Derek caught his breath and went still for a moment, then rapidly discarded his shirt and kicked off the soft-soled moccasins he always wore. "I'm glad," he said with rough-edged gentleness. "Because I want you too, honey."

Shannon's gaze went over his body, curiously half-primitive clad only in jeans, and the wonder in her grew. He was so beautiful, so stunningly male. So perfect. The thick mat of hair on his broad chest was gold-tipped, both soft and rough to her touch, arrowing down his hard stomach and disappearing beneath the waistband of his jeans. Muscles rippled with every movement, catching the light, and the sheer power of him was a palpable force that stirred her senses wildly.

And the warmth of him . . . the wonderful, seductive warmth of him. She went into his arms as though drawn by a lodestar, wanting him, needing him and the warmth he'd created in them both. Impatient, she wanted the barriers gone, wanted to feel him against her. She lifted her face to meet the heat of his kiss, barely able to hold herself away from him long enough to allow him the room to unfasten her silken pajama top. She shrugged out of the top and instantly pressed against him, gasping at the intimate contact as the tips of her breasts turned to fire, seduced by her own body's response to the hardness of his. Her hands found the ridged firmness of his stomach, and she felt muscles contract beneath her touch.

"Nobody told me," she said shakily as he lifted his head and looked down at her with his dark, hot eyes. "Nobody told me it felt like this."

Derek wanted to tell her that, in his experience, it didn't feel like this. Not like this. Nothing had ever felt like this. For the first time, he truly understood why Kelsey, one of the strongest men he'd ever known, had all but come apart in the turbulence of love and need. Derek knew what it felt like now, and he wondered on some distant level of his mind if he would be able to survive this intact. Something shuddered inside him. He didn't think he would.

He had already lost something, given it to her. Or perhaps she had stolen it, taken it from him in her innocent need. It was gone, hers, and he'd never get it back again.

"Derek—?"

He realized he'd gone very still, and wondered if the sudden ferocity he felt showed on his face. His eyes searched her lovely, awakened face, gazed in fascination at the pulse beating rapidly in her throat, and then lowered to the pale gold mounds of her breasts. "You're beautiful, Shannon," he murmured tautly. "Lord, you're so beautiful!" His hands found the waistband of her pajama bottoms, and he began drawing them downward as he bent his head and kissed her shoulder.

One of Shannon's hands left his stomach, capturing his left wrist with jerky quickness as she caught her breath suddenly and stiffened.

Derek raised his head and looked into amber eyes that skittered nervously away from his intent gaze for the first time. And he knew, even before the whispered words escaped her.

"The light . . . turn it off, please, Derek. I don't want you to see—the accident . . . there were operations, and I don't want you to see." Her eyes were changing, darkening, a new kind of awareness bringing a sanity that was cold and afraid.

The lamplight from the lower level was barely enough to illuminate the bed and them. Barely enough. But enough for her to be afraid of what he'd see. Derek knew that it could end right here. She could stop him now, and would, given only a moment in his own hesitation to think. But if it ended here and now, he knew it would be over for good. Because Shannon would always remember the moment it ended. And why it ended.

"The light," she whispered, a hint of desperation in her unsteady voice. "Derek, the light—"

"Shhh." He kept his hands still at her waist while his lips feathered over her face, down her throat. He explored the flushed curves of her breasts with gentle hunger, hearing the kittenlike sound she made in the back of her throat, and felt both her hands lift to his neck as he dropped slowly to one knee. The sensitive flesh of her stomach quivered beneath his lips, and this time there was no resistance when he slid the pajamas down over her curved hips and slender legs.

Still, he felt her stiffen, felt the sudden fearful, waiting tension in her as the scars became visible to him. He hurt when he saw the pain she had endured, saw what had been done to her. One scar curved over her hip joint, the wide, pale mark of an incision to repair inner damage. A second scar tracked down her upper thigh, several inches long and jagged. And there were other, fainter marks, wounds made by glass or metal, injuries that had marked a soul as well as a body.

Derek touched the scars with infinite gentleness, tracing each one with a sensitive finger and then his lips. He felt as well as heard the sob that caught at her as tension drained away, and her body seemed to curve briefly over his in a posture that was grateful and curiously protective.

"Ugly," she whispered. "So ugly."

"No." He rose slowly back to his feet, one hand stroking her hip with a soft touch. He could taste the salt of her tears when he kissed her, and his free hand drew her close. "Not ugly. Just a part of you, honey. And you're beautiful."

Shannon caught her breath when he lifted her and placed her in the center of the turned-down bed. She lay gazing up at him as he discarded what remained of his clothing, and some distant part of her wondered if this could possibly be happening. She looked at him, powerful and starkly masculine, his body painted a dark bronze by the lamplight. She should have been afraid of so much power, so much perfect beauty—and then she saw the scar on his upper thigh, a jagged, twisting mark. A new kind of shock rippled through her. Not perfect. Scarred like her.

Derek came down on the bed beside her, taking her hand and guiding it to touch the scar he bore. "We all have scars, honey," he said softly, roughly. "Inside or out—or both. We all have scars."

She could feel the puckered flesh beneath her fingers, familiar to her touch because her scars felt like that, and she looked at him wonderingly. In that moment, she had never felt so close to another human being. And then she became aware of the hardness of his body as he half leaned over her, and she forgot about scars. Her hands lifted, one touching his powerful chest and the other sliding up his spine, and her mouth responded instantly, wildly, to the touch of his.

She was burning out of control, caught up in something that left her dizzy and breathless and needing. There was no time to think, and the time for questioning these turbulent new needs was long in the past. She barely heard the hungry sound that escaped her when his lips left hers to burn a trail down her throat. Tension was winding inside her like a spring, tighter and tighter.

His own need was coiling inside him, and Derek was jarred by the unfamiliar possessiveness of that inner beast. He watched his hands at her breasts, large and bronzed against her pale golden flesh, watched her rosy nipples harden with every teasing stroke of his fingers. His gaze flicked up to her face, flushed and awakened, the tender lips faintly swollen from his passion and the big amber eyes heavy-lidded with desire. And when the realization and acceptance of it flashed through his mind with brilliant clarity, a broken sound escaped from somewhere deep inside him and he buried his face between her breasts.

His. She was his. His heart, his soul, the other half of him. He had known he loved her, but he hadn't known until that moment just how terribly vital she was to his very existence.

"Derek."

He kept his gaze fixed on her body even as he lifted his head, unwilling to let her see what he knew was blazing out of him through his eyes. If his own violent emotions scared the hell out of him, what would they do to her? He couldn't risk it. The gamble he was already taking by making love to her now was dangerous enough.

He concentrated on her breasts again, tasting her soft skin, gliding his tongue slowly around a hardened bud that begged mutely for a closer caress. He heard her whimper when his mouth closed at last over her nipple, and the choked little cry was the most seductive sound he'd ever heard. He could feel his own body respond wildly, feel the pounding pulse of his desire throb harder, stronger, until it seemed there was nothing left of him but that madly escalating need.

It was all he could do to hang on to some kind of control, and it took every shred of strength he could command to hold back when he wanted to bury himself in her, possess her until they were fused, bonded, until she'd never be rid of him. Only the knowledge that she was a virgin, a knowledge that was as sure as his own love, kept him in control. And it was because he loved her that he felt the weight of that responsibility so strongly: if she were hurt or frightened in this first vital joining, she could be forever beyond his reach.

However she felt about him in the morning, Derek wanted her memories of tonight to hold nothing but pleasure.

His mouth moved from one breast to the other,

and his hand slid down her side, pausing for a moment to gently rub the scarred hip she was no longer aware of. He felt the slender tautness of her thigh, the skin like silk, and eased his hand to the inside, just above her knees. Her legs were pressed together, and he could feel the instinctive resistance in tightening muscles. But he was patient, slow, aware that her breath was coming faster and that her body's needs were overcoming instinct.

Shannon felt his touch easing her legs apart, and something panicky stirred in her mind. She caught her breath to voice some protest, but then her pounding heart seemed to lodge in her throat and block the words before they could emerge. She was hot, burning, and her body didn't want to be still, couldn't be still. His mouth on her breasts was feeding the fire, the swirling tongue maddening, and the heat spread in waves until she thought she'd burst into flames.

Her nails dug unconsciously into his back, and she distantly heard a ragged moan, only vaguely aware that the sound came from her, that her legs were parting for him, obeying his insistent touch. That caressing hand was moving closer, closer, trailing more fire in its wake. She felt an awful, empty ache, and some new instinct told her he could make the ache go away, fill the emptiness. And then she caught her breath again as his gentle fingers settled over the pulsing ache, some animal sound fighting to escape her taut throat.

"Derek!" The animal sound, his name torn from her in a surge of violent need.

"So soft and warm," he murmured hoarsely

against her breast, the vibration of his words a new caress. His fingers probed her softness slowly and thoroughly, a building caress that stole her breath and shocked her senses, until she was trembling, until another ragged moan escaped her and her body moved in restless urgency to his touch. "You're so beautiful you're driving me out of my mind."

Shannon thought she was going out of her mind, and her body was a disconnected thing filled with heat and need and a tension spiraling out of control. She was throbbing in a quickening rhythm, every inch of her pulsing in a single, giant heartbeat of desire. She felt the coiling tension wind tighter, felt all her senses rushing toward some distant explosion, and she wanted the detonation to swallow her up, engulf her, vanquish her.

But when the explosion came, it was triumph rather than defeat, lifting her in a violent rush to some distant place that was nothing but mind-numbing pleasure. She hadn't known such feelings were possible, and the wonder nearly stopped her heart.

The calm that finally descended over her was a fleeting thing, because Derek's caresses began building tension again. Dazed, she felt the return of that slow, throbbing pulse inside her, and the strength of renewed need flowed back into her boneless limbs. Caught up in what was happening, she was only vaguely aware that he had paused briefly to reach into the nightstand drawer, and even though her mind understood what he was doing, she wasn't troubled by the ramifications of his action.

She caught her breath when he moved over her,

feeling an instant's panic, a smothering sensation because he was so big and blotted out the light, because she felt so vulnerable. But then he was kissing her deeply, hungrily, and panic vanished. Her legs cradled him, and she felt a hard, blunt pressure, gentle but insistent. She caught at his shoulders as he raised his head, a distant echo of shock passing through her at the instinctive feminine realization of an alien intruder.

His face. She was mesmerized by his face. It was taut, hard, beautiful. Primitive, as if all the civilized layers had been stripped away from him by need. His dark eyes blazed down at her, and she saw now that the curious flecks of color were a deep, rich blue, sapphire glints in the darkness they shone out of. She felt an odd, jarring surprise when she realized that, a strange intensity of emotion that washed over her in a hard wave.

"I don't want to hurt you, sweetheart," he said thickly, braced above her in tense stillness, feverish eyes fixed on her face.

And in that moment, without thought, she trusted him in the most simple, intimate, primitive way a woman could ever trust a man. With no hesitation, she trusted him with her vulnerability. The smile that curved her lips was as old as the caves.

Derek almost groaned aloud when he saw that trust shining in her amber eyes, and understood what it meant. It was more than he had dared to hope for, and his heart lurched when she offered it willingly. He could destroy that trust if he hurt her, he knew. But if trust remained intact when the morning and the world intruded, that slender but tempered steel bond forged in the blazing heat of their passion could very well turn out to be his only lifeline.

"Shannon," he whispered, lowering his head to kiss her very tenderly.

"You won't hurt me," she murmured, her arms encircling his neck as she sought to draw him down to her.

Derek did groan then, and it was a rough sound edged with harsh strain as he fought to control his ravening need for her. He moved with exquisite care, gritting his teeth at the sheer pleasure of entering her body with such restraint. The searing tightness of her was a caress that sent his senses spinning wildly, snatching at his control until he felt torn in two, rent by the terrible conflict of savage need and tender love.

Shannon could see that conflict in his face, even as her body struggled to adjust to his slow possession. She could feel the instinctive shock of her body, the resistance, but there was no pain. He was filling her, stretching her, satisfying the emptiness that had ached for him. A momentary intruder, he became a part of her so smoothly that her body accepted him totally.

Derek was still, his breathing a rasping sound, searching her face intently for any sign of pain. "Shannon?" he whispered.

She looked up at him with wide, awed eyes, and her arms tightened slowly around his neck as she felt the throbbing power of him deep inside her. "I'm . . . fine," she murmured after searching briefly for another word, a better word to tell him how wonderful she felt. Without her volition, her body moved, lifting to have more of him as tension coiled and demanded again.

A harsh sound escaped from Derek as his body responded instantly to her. He wanted to be careful and every muscle was tense with the effort as he answered her movements with his own, setting up a slow rhythm that escalated swiftly beyond any control he could have claimed. Her body sheathed his with a molten tightness that seared away caution, and her equally wild response drove both of them past the limits of mastery.

Shannon gloried in his strength and hers, meeting his increasingly powerful thrusts with her own lithe force as the hot, spiraling tension coiled inside her. His fiery kisses possessed her even as his body did, demanding, hungry, taking her. And she took as well, insisting with a woman's silent, soul-deep need that he be hers, at least for tonight.

The firestorm of passion swept over them both, catching them, flinging them savagely into a bottomless well of mindless pleasure that tore a wordless cry from her and a rasping groan from him, joining them in an instant, making them one in that brief, timeless interlude that occurs only rarely between mortals.

Shannon came back to the awareness of her existence as a separate being very slowly, and the heavy heat of his body over hers helped ease the shock of transition. In a moment of clarity, she realized that never, as long as she lived, would she forget that brief, stark instant of sharing. Her trembling hands moved over his powerful back and shoulders, and she smiled when he lifted his head to gaze down at her.

Derek eased up onto his elbows, and his hands

framed her face gently. One thumb brushed the swollen curve of her lower lip, and a slight frown drew his brows together. "Was I too rough, sweetheart? A didn't want to be." His voice was husky.

Shannon's smile widened. "No." She lifted a hand to touch his cheek. "No."

He wanted to ask: Was it a mistake? But he didn't. He knew that only the morning, and the mornings to follow, would answer the question. He turned his head to kiss her soft palm, and then sought her lips almost blindly, wishing he could stop time, stop the world. Wishing he could transport them both instantly to some deserted island where no one would bother them and she wouldn't be able to run away from him when morning came.

"Derek?" She was a little puzzled, a little anxious, bothered by something she felt in him, something that seemed alien to what she knew of him. Derek afraid? No. No, not him.

He smiled suddenly, those sapphire-flecked dark eyes glowing down at her. "You're so lovely, Shannon."

And she smiled slowly in return, forgetting anxiety. For once, just this once, she believed him. "Thank you."

Still smiling, he eased away from her and got them both under the covers, making her giggle because he mildly cursed a stubborn blanket, and because he very solemnly arranged them both beneath the covers so that he could hold her "just right" during the night.

Shannon fell asleep still smiling, cradled in his arms, listening to his heart beat.

She woke twice in the night to the vague thought that he certainly wasn't getting the rest he needed, but not about to protest his renewed desire. Both times he assumed responsibility for their love-making, and both times she took note of that without thinking about it very much. She was too wrapped up in the fire he ignited to allow for much thinking.

Even in the heat of passion, Shannon had known morning would come, and that she would have to face him and herself, have to accept and understand what she had done. But she wasn't prepared for morning to arrive with a breathless shock of interruption that cut them apart with the deadly swiftness of a knife.

She felt Derek move before she heard anything, and the tension she sensed in him brought her wide awake. She was sitting up even as he slid from the bed, clutching the sheet to her breasts and blinking in a sudden awareness of the soft buzzing sound that was coming from a little box she hadn't noticed on the nightstand at his side of the bed.

That nightstand, she thought vaguely. Damn that nightstand. She wondered idly why she was damning the unoffending piece of furniture, but she wasn't ready to think about consequences yet, and the subject escaped her.

"Derek?" It was a whisper, a plea for him to tell her everything was all right.

He didn't answer. She wasn't even sure he heard her. Face taut and expressionless, unconcerned with or even unaware of his nakedness, he moved swiftly and silently to the rolltop desk, opening it to reveal two portable television sets where the cubbyholes should have been. He turned both on, and Shannon caught a glimpse of grainy pictures, shadows and gray light and stealthy movements. It was only in the instant he moved aside and reached to turn the sets off that she recognized in the pictures the front of the building they were in.

"Get dressed, Shannon." His voice was soft and hard at the same time. "We have company. It'll take them awhile to get through the downstairs doors—we'll slip out while they're busy with that."

She slid from the bed instantly, aware of a leaden coldness filling her. And, as he began swiftly gathering his clothes and dressing, she felt a wave of embarrassment at her own nudity. Her hands seemed to be all thumbs, and she concentrated fiercely on what she was doing, shoving her pajamas into the bag Derek had given her and snatching out underthings, jeans, and a thick sweater. Her eyes were burning and her throat hurt, and she dressed with shaking hands.

Morning had arrived.

Derek wanted to reassure her, and the bitterness of what was happening tore at him. It was *wrong*. They should have had time, time to be lovers. He could have helped her ease into the unfamiliar situation, could have avoided the tense embarrassment he saw in her averted face. Instead, she was being jerked rudely from their bed, and the cold necessity of that was hurting her in a way no woman should ever be hurt.

And there was nothing he could do about it.

There was no time to make it easier for her. He couldn't even go to her and hold her, because there was no time. He silently, viciously damned the man responsible, and knew that if he ever got his hands around the bastard's neck he'd choke the life out of him.

"I'm ready." Her voice was soft, toneless. She had sat on the bed to pull on socks and running shoes, and now stood and reached for her packed bag.

Derek took it from her, holding hers and his own in one hand. His free arm encircled her abruptly, and he hugged her hard. "It's all right, sweetheart," he promised quietly, making an effort even over the urgency he felt not to sound as sharp and businesslike as before. "Everything's going to be all right."

"Yes. I know." Her voice was still toneless, and she wouldn't look at him.

No time. Dammit, no time! He led her to the closet and his escape hatch, guiding her firmly, instructing her when necessary. They were soon moving quietly through a narrow tunnel lighted only by the flashlight he carried.

Idly, Shannon counted their steps; she had reached fifty when they made a right turn. Fifty more steps and they had reached a ladder. Obeying his low-voiced command, she waited at the bottom of the steps, holding the flashlight, until he came back for her. Then she followed him up.

They emerged inside a building crowded with unidentifiable machinery, hulking in shadows. A gray dawn light struggled to penetrate the high, dirty windows. The flashlight had been left behind them in the tunnel and Shannon could hardly see, but Derek was holding her hand and that was enough. She felt numb.

Derek had started toward what seemed to be a door, but he stopped suddenly, and she could feel his tension, could literally feel his senses flaring out in a sudden probing search. And Shannon wasn't really surprised to see a tall figure step from behind some of the machinery, because Derek had somehow known he was there.

"It's been a long time, Derek." The man's voice was low, calm but guarded.

Six

Shannon still felt Derek's tension, but it was lessening, or somehow different, and his voice was soft and guarded as well.

"Prague, wasn't it?"

A quiet laugh came from the tall man. "You left me in a very difficult situation, my friend."

"The fortunes of war, Alexi," Derek responded a bit dryly.

"Yes. And how well we know them, eh?"

There was a moment of silence, and then Derek said, "You aren't with them." It was a statement of fact.

"No," the man named Alexi agreed.

"How did you find this?"

The man took the question literally, as Derek had obviously intended. "You always plan a way out. This seemed the most likely spot."

Derek nodded. "I see."

There was another silence, and then the man said, "I need a white flag, Derek."

"All right." Derek's agreement was instant. "When and where?"

"There is a park a mile west of your apartment. A gazebo by the lake. In three hours."

Derek inclined his head slightly. "I'll be there."

Without another word, the man melted back into the shadows. And Derek never even glanced toward those shadows as he led Shannon past them and out of the building.

He was still holding her hand, guiding her firmly between two more buildings, down an alley, across a street. He said nothing, and Shannon, bewildered by his terse, cryptic exchange with the strange man, remained silent as well.

Still numb, she felt suspended, as if nothing that was happening was real. This wasn't the man who had trembled with need in the night, the man who had made love to her so tenderly and passionately. This was another man, a terse, impersonal man with an animal's instincts for danger and a professional's instant response to that danger.

And she wasn't, she realized with a sense of grief, the woman who had given herself so passionately. That woman belonged to the night, had fled in the gray light of morning. She was just Shannon again, alone and afraid. Or was she? There was something more now, she thought, something different. But she was too numb to try to understand.

They walked a careful path in shadows between buildings for nearly half an hour, until Derek stopped by another somewhat battered car. Detached, she watched him unlock the door, and asked mildly, "Just how many cars do you have, anyway?"

He looked down at her, hesitated, and then shrugged. "A few. Get in, honey."

She got in. When he had stowed their bags in the back and gotten in as well, she idly watched his long-fingered, powerful hands at the wheel of the car. Such strong hands. "Are we going to another one of your burrows?" she asked.

After a moment, he said, "Yes. Another one. Shannon, I'm sorry this happened. I didn't think they'd find us so quickly. If we'd had a few more days—"

"How many burrows do you have?"

Derek was automatically concentrating on driving, and shot her a quick look. She didn't seem to be withdrawn so much as just not there. It worried him. "A few. Shannon—"

"A few cars. A few burrows. And a girl in every port, I suppose." She seemed distantly amused. "Mixing my metaphors. Who was that man?"

He ignored the question. "It didn't change anything between us, honey. I want you."

"You had me," she murmured.

The look he sent her this time was hard. "Don't say that. As if it didn't matter. As if it were just—"

"Sex?" She shook her head, puzzled by him or by herself, or by what they were saying to each other. "Where are we going?"

Derek decided to drop it for now: Shannon wasn't in any condition for this. "A house," he answered, sighing.

"Yours," she noted. "Like the apartment and

the loft and the other burrows and cars and women. Yours."

He didn't respond, falling silent and remaining that way. It was another half hour before he turned the car into the driveway of a semi-secluded house, not small or particularly large, just neat and rather—homey. Shannon thought the word both apt and ridiculous: Apt because that's what it pretended to be, and ridiculous because it was a burrow.

There was an automatic garage-door opener in the car—of course, she thought—and Derek drove the car in, closing the door behind it. She got out without being told to and followed him from the garage into the house, also not surprised to see him unlock the door. There were a number of keys on that ring he carried. She had a fleeting vision of burrows and cars stretching into infinity, and swallowed a giggle.

It was better than being embarrassed.

The house was decorated the way houses usually were, with furniture and things. Nothing too shabby or too expensive, and nothing out of place in its surroundings. A nice, homey little house-burrow. She knew the refrigerator and cabinets would be stocked, the beds made with fresh linen. It must cost him a bundle, she thought, to keep himself in ready burrows. Another giggle locked behind her teeth.

She wasn't stupid. She recognized hysteria when it was trying to get her by the throat. She was rather proud of herself for not giving in to it. Well, not completely giving in to it.

"Shannon." Derek dropped their bags in the middle of a cosy living room and turned to face her, grasping her shoulders firmly. "Are you all right?"

She debated how to answer that. And she must have debated too long, because he shook her gently. "Why wouldn't I be all right?" she asked finally as a sort of compromise.

"Shannon—"

Something broke. He broke it with his rough, unsteady voice saying her name, with his nearness, with his sapphire-flecked eyes. He broke it. She didn't know what it was that had broken, and she didn't really care, but suddenly she was crying in painful sobs that shook her entire body. Crying, and in his arms, holding on to him, to his warmth and strength, barely aware of his crooning voice.

At some point, she became aware that she was weeping like a rainy sky and drenching his shirt, aware that she was clutching him as if he could save her from drowning in her own tears. She tried to push herself away from him in that moment of conscious understanding, but he wouldn't let go of her.

Finally, she was spent, and felt unsettled to discover they were on a couch. Or that, more specifically, he was on the couch and she was on his lap. She felt like a tearful child after a tantrum. The feeling increased when he produced a hankerchief and ordered her gently to blow her nose. She felt a little mutinous, but blew. Then she sat bolt upright on his lap and glared at him.

"I wasn't hysterical," she announced with a firmness only slightly marred by a stray sniffle.

He was studying her face intently, a frown of worry drawing his brows together, but at this masterly inaccuracy the frown vanished and a gleam of laughter was born in his eyes. "No, of course not," he agreed gravely.

"Don't humor me!" she snapped. The feeling of rebellious childishness grew. She didn't like it.

The amusement remained in the curve of his smile, but his eyes were intent again, searching. "Shannon, you had every right to be hysterical," he told her quietly. "I was afraid you'd try to keep it bottled up inside you, instead of letting go. What happened this morning would have driven any sane woman over the edge. You should never have been hurt like that."

She avoided his gaze suddenly. He'd gotten too close last night, but it was morning now and she couldn't let him get that close again. There was too much potential hurt in his closeness. On the point of withdrawing emotionally, she saw abruptly that she was sitting in his lap and her feet wouldn't reach the floor, and it annoyed her.

She felt . . . strange. Wary, guarded. But he was *there* somehow, too close to push away. She couldn't lock her emotions away anymore; they were all confused in her mind, and she couldn't get hold of them. And there was something else inside her, something new and different. Something tough. And she wondered suddenly if the explosive passion of last night had changed her in some way she could only sense.

"Shannon? Honey, I'm sorry we had to leave so suddenly like that. But it *didn't* change anything between us. I still want you, more than ever—"

"No." She hadn't even realized until then that she was going to say it.

Derek was very still. "No, what?" he asked steadily. "No, I don't want you? No, you don't want me? Or no, it was just a one-night stand?"

She wanted to hide from his questions, but couldn't. This time, she couldn't. Looking fixedly at the fingers twined together in her lap, she said softly, "You said it would be a mistake for us to—to—"

"Make love," he supplied harshly.

Shannon winced. "Yes. You said it would be a mistake, that the timing was wrong. And you were right. It shouldn't have happened." She could feel as well as hear him draw a deep breath before responding.

"But it did happen, Shannon. And you wanted me as much as I wanted you."

"I can't deny that." She flushed as she remembered her abandoned passion of last night. Had that really been *her*? "I'm not blaming you. But it was too much, just as you said it would be. I can't think." She hesitated, then said almost inaudibly, "It would be so easy to stop thinking. Because last night I forgot everything but you and the way you made me feel. But I can't let that happen again, Derek."

After a moment, Derek reached out a big hand to cover both of hers. "I was afraid something like this would happen." His voice was quiet, rough-edged. "That's why I wanted to wait." He hesitated, then said steadily, "Shannon, you've been through a hell of a lot the last few days, and I don't want to push you. But no matter what, don't forget that I care about you, all right? No matter what happens, no matter how confusing everything is or becomes, count on my feelings for you."

"All right." But she slipped from his lap before he could stop her, moving away to sit in a chair near the couch. She felt like crying again for some reason, and determinedly changed the subject. "Who was that man? And what did he mean by a white flag? A truce of some kind?"

Derek was reluctant to leave things as they were—an emotional mine field where an unwary step could destroy both of them—but knew he had no choice. She hadn't completely withdrawn from him; he was thankful for that. Her guarded wariness was a natural reaction, and even if it did hurt him, it was not unexpected. There was nothing he could do except be as patient as he knew how until she worked everything out for herself.

"That man is Alexi. He's sometimes a friend. Usually an enemy."

Her eyes widened. "What—"

"He's Russian, Shannon."

She blinked. "Oh." She couldn't think of a better reaction to that startling bit of information. "Is he a part of what's happening at Civatech?"

"He says not; you heard him. He's not with them. 'Them' meaning the ones we were getting away from. But he followed us from the apartment to the loft."

"How do you know that?"

"Makes sense. He couldn't have found it any other way. He doesn't have the connections here to find every buried deed with my name on it."

Shannon was confused. "But if he isn't involved, why did he show up?"

"He wants to talk."

"Is that what a white flag means?"

Derek nodded and leaned his head back against

the couch. "There are rules," he explained slowly. "Even between enemies. Maybe especially between enemies. A white flag is a truce always honored. It *has* to be honored by both sides, because none of us can work completely without rules."

She shook her head, thinking of the dangers of that kind of trust between enemies. "But it sounds perfect for some kind of setup," she offered.

"Of course it is," he said frankly. "And that's why a white flag has to be honored. If an agent offered a truce and then broke it, word would spread through the intelligence community like wildfire. That agent could never be trusted again. By either side."

"A question of integrity?"

"Maybe. And maybe it's just a core of sanity in an insane business."

Shannon thought it over. "So Alexi is sort of your counterpart? An agent for the Russians?"

He nodded.

"Do you think he followed us here?"

"No."

He sounded so sure, and Shannon looked at him doubtfully. "How can you be certain?"

Derek smiled a little. "Another sort of rule. Alexi had a string on either me or you—we can't know which yet, but he was watching one of us. He followed us to the loft, and kept a close eye on the place. But by coming out into the open and asking for a meet, he cut the string, stopped the surveillance. It was meant to be understood by us that he wouldn't follow this time."

She had a sudden flash of intuition, and wondered if she could possibly be right. There was more here. "Derek, you said he was sometimes a friend."

"Yes."

"How could he be? He's an enemy agent."

After a moment, Derek said soberly, "Ideologies don't mean much in the field. Governments aren't always practical, but agents have to be. Sometimes there are common goals, Shannon. And sometimes the best way to achieve those goals is by hanging out a white flag and working shoulder-to-shoulder with your enemy."

"You like him," she said softly.

He smiled. "I like him, yes. I respect him. And I regret the necessity of living in a world where he and I can't be friends . . . all the time."

Shannon chewed her bottom lip. "It's more than that, though, isn't it?"

Derek's smile widened. "You're very perceptive. It might be wishful thinking on my part, but I've more than once suspected Alexi could be a double agent."

"Working for both sides?"

"Primarily for ours, I'd like to think. There have been a few occasions—" He abruptly rose to his feet, stretching his muscular arms. "It's a crazy game," he murmured, then apparently shook off the thought. "We have time for breakfast. And then we have to go and meet our—enemy."

She got up, gazing at him hesitantly. "We?"

He caught her hand and carried it briefly to his lips. "We. I told you. I want you with me. I won't leave you alone, no matter what."

The comment was light and casual, but his eyes were something else. Shannon allowed herself to be led toward the kitchen, struggling with a sudden pulsing awareness of him.

Had she been blind to him before last night? She'd been aware of him, yes, but not like this. Was it because they had been, however briefly, lovers? Never before in her life had she been so conscious of a man's body, of his blatant sexuality. That look in his eyes had been intent, somber . . . and more. She'd felt a sudden heat, a vibrant awakening of all her senses as if he'd touched her physically the way he had last night, with hunger and passion.

She hadn't counted on that. It had seemed so simple in the sane light of morning. Just stop it, stop it all. No complicated physical relationship and so—no problem. It hadn't occurred to her that her own body and senses could betray her. She hadn't realized she would be fighting herself.

But she was awake, really for the first time in her life. He had awakened her.

And as she looked at him now, watched him move about the kitchen with efficient grace and seemingly unaware of her gaze, she felt those awakened senses fill with him. He seemed to . . . radiate heat and power. She wanted to touch him, wanted to feel the fine golden hairs of his forearm under her fingers. She wanted to press her suddenly aching body against his, bury her face against him and inhale the pleasing musky scent she remembered so vividly.

She wanted to feel his hands on her, stopping her breath, his mouth arousing her to the incredible heights of ecstasy he had taught her to feel. She wanted *him*.

Shannon drew a deep, silent breath, shaken.

Her heart, that physical organ, pounded against her ribs. But the emotional organ that was also her heart lay solidly protected beneath the layers of pain and wariness that years had built.

Her heart was safe, she thought. Safe. Safe from pain. Safe from him. Her body would betray her before her heart did.

Zach Steele leaned forward to point to the computer printout in front of him on the coffee table, glancing at his companions. "Civatech has a regularly scheduled shipping point in Norfolk. They transport overland that far, and then load the ship—it's theirs, by the way—and just sail out. They sell their toys overseas to our allies, so what's to stop them shipping out this device along with the rest?"

Josh, sitting on the couch across from his friend and security expert, grimaced faintly. "What about the naval base?"

Zach shrugged. "Everything's inspected before it leaves port. But what're they looking at, Josh? That's the question. Disassemble any electronic device and it's just a lot of spare parts. And even if they ship it in one piece, who's to know what it is? They could probably label it some kind of computer on the invoice, and nobody'd be the wiser."

Raven, sitting on the floor with her back against the couch, frowned thoughtfully. "So, once they were out of U.S. waters, they could meet that tanker of Yaltan's and just hand the device over to him."

Zach nodded. "Easy as pie. It's Civatech's ship, and Adam Moreton has the authority to divert it temporarily. The news about the tanker being turned back isn't public, so the captain and crew probably wouldn't suspect the neutral flag."

Raven was chewing on a thumbnail. "In other words, once they get that device to Norfolk, it's pretty much gone."

"Unless somebody stops it," Josh noted. "Zach, does Civatech ship overland by the same route every time?"

With one of his smiles that could easily frighten someone who didn't know him, Zach nodded. "Regular as clockwork. And they wouldn't want to vary the routine now. They average two trucks leaving Richmond every time they ship, which is twice a week. The next shipment is due to leave Norfolk the day after tomorrow, Friday. So two trucks are likely to leave Civatech tomorrow. Sure as hell, one's going to contain an innocent shipment—and one won't."

They looked at one another for a moment, and then Raven sighed. "Derek needs to know. His only chance is to waylay that truck somehow."

"We could go public," Zach suggested. "Let the military or state police deal with it."

Josh gave him a look. "On what evidence? It might take days, maybe weeks, for the police to put everything together. There is such a thing as due process, you know."

Mildly, Raven said. "Zach, if you don't think it's safe for Josh to get involved openly, then he won't. You know that."

The big security expert stirred uneasily. "Luc found more evidence of tampering," he said abruptly, referring to the chief investigator for Long Enterprises. "Your apartment. They hadn't had time to finish the job, but . . ."

Raven turned her head to look soberly at her husband. "That's it, then."

"No, it damn well isn't it," Josh said. "I'll take reasonable precautions, but I won't hide inside a cage. Besides, all the attempts and threats have been in New York—there hasn't been a whisper here. And I haven't exactly been out of the public eye with the strike threatening. If somebody had wanted to get to me, they could have."

After a moment, Raven looked back at Zach. "So."

He nodded reluctantly. His friend of more than fifteen years was a man who didn't like to be backed into corners, and Zach had learned when to stop pushing. "All right. So how do we get in touch with Derek?"

Josh looked at his wife, smiling faintly.

"Where there's a will," she said, "there's a way."

The gazebo was a round, white little structure with built-in benches inside along the waist-high rails. It sat at the edge of a small lake where ducks swam, and it was deserted except for a tall man who was casually dressed and who lounged back on one of the benches, idly smoking a cigarette.

Shannon was grateful for Derek's strong hand holding hers, even though she felt that his trust in the other man had likely been hard-earned over years of situations like this one, and that she could count on Derek's instincts. Still, she felt a little nervous. She wondered vaguely and a bit uncomfortably about her own prejudices, wondered if her feelings were unconsciously based on propaganda.

But then Alexi rose politely as they stepped up into the gazebo, and Shannon knew that her uneasiness had little to do with "ideologies."

He was as tall as Derek, black-haired, and with an athletic build. Probably, like Derek, he was in his mid-thirties. His face was handsome in a rather cold way, and his eyes so light gray they seemed almost colorless. And it was those eyes Shannon saw and felt, those eyes and the danger in them.

"Your partner?" Derek asked as they sat down across from the other man.

Alexi smiled faintly. "Watching."

Derek nodded, unsurprised and accepting, but Shannon felt the hair on the nape of her neck rise. She'd never liked being stared at, and the sensation of being watched now disturbed her. Still holding her hand, Derek squeezed it gently, and she realized he was aware of her feelings.

"Still Gina?" He asked Alexi.

"Still."

Derek smiled a little. "When are you going to marry her?"

Without hesitation, and in the same tone his counterpart had used, Alexi replied, "When she recovers from the idea that she's in love with you."

Shannon felt a jarring shock, and when she looked at Derek she saw he was honestly surprised.

"I didn't know," he said finally.

Alexi laughed almost soundlessly. "No. How could you? You've seen her—what?—half a dozen times in as many years? And, to be fair, you must have looked very much like a white knight to her on those occasions. It was inevitable. She hasn't quite lost her romantic view of this business, our Gina. She will soon." His last comment was made flatly, and the colorless eyes brooded for an instant.

Shannon could feel Derek's sudden alertness, and tried herself to tap into the undercurrents she was dimly aware of. There was something more here, she sensed, but she couldn't begin to grasp what it was.

Derek didn't say anything; he just watched the other man steadily. When Alexi met that calm gaze, his own eyes lost the brooding look and smiled.

"The sun always sets in the west," he said lightly.

"End run," Derek murmured.

"End run. Much more unexpected." Alexi was silent for a moment, and then his gaze flicked to Shannon's puzzled face. "I followed Miss Brown to your apartment." His voice was brisk now, businesslike. "Discovering it *was* yours was a bit unexpected—but not unwelcome."

"So it was Civatech you were on?"

"Yes. Via a Middle Eastern route. Word reached us some weeks ago that a certain fanatical enemy of both of our countries had been contacted through an intermediary to discuss the purchase of a rather extraordinary device. He couldn't, of course, conquer the world, as he wishes to, with this weapon alone, but it would be an important addition to his arsenal. And if he managed to manufacture a number of the devices, he might upset the balance of power."

Derek didn't react to the information with any change of expression, he merely asked, "And how did you get onto Shannon?"

Alexi seemed to debate for a silent moment before saying, "It was simple to discover that Miss Brown took care of Adam Moreton's correspondence when his personal secretary was absent. Miss Brown's office is in the unrestricted section of the building, unlike Moreton's secretary's office. The obvious means to gain access to that correspondence was to temporarily remove his secretary so that Miss Brown would handle it—in her unrestricted and accessible office."

"You didn't hurt her?" Shannon burst out, horrified.

Alexi smiled. "Moreton's secretary? No, Miss Brown. In point of fact, though she called in sick, she's entirely well. Just rather . . . involved with a handsome young attorney."

"Neat," Derek commented.

Alexi inclined his head slightly. "And simple. He is, of course, one of ours. He was initially somewhat disgusted to find that after years of training his task was to merely be himself and make love to a woman. But she is a rather beautiful woman, so I doubt he still considers it a hardship."

If anything, Shannon was even more horrified. People as pawns. She was beginning to understand that the world she had stumbled into held layers upon layers of deception. "That's terrible," she whispered.

Alexi glanced at her, a flicker of sympathy softening his hard eyes. "She won't suffer, Miss Brown," he said gently. "The initial meeting was planned cold-bloodedly, but humans are just humans, after all. They are merely two people who met, as is always the case. She may fall in love. He may fall in love. And we may avert a crisis."

"So the end justifies the means?" she asked tightly.

He nodded slowly, still holding her gaze. "Always, it comes to that question. And the answer is: If the end is to prevent a war that could kill millions horribly, then almost any means can be justified. And if one heart his broken, then the only sadness is she won't know that what cost her so much spared so many others unimaginable pain."

Shannon didn't know quite how to respond to that, and her eyes fell before Alexi's steady gaze. She suddenly wondered how many times Derek had been forced to make a choice that had broken a heart, or cost a life, to spare others or to avert something terrible.

Derek had listened silently, without comment, to the discussion. "So," he said finally, "Shannon was Moreton's secretary. And a lot more accessible. What then?"

Alexi chuckled suddenly. "For a high-tech company as security-conscious as Civatech, they made a basic mistake. Miss Brown types correspondence on a simple electric typewriter."

"The ribbon," Derek guessed. "A film ribbon?"

"A film ribbon. It was simple to slip in near the end of the day when Miss Brown took her letters away for the proper signatures, and replace the ribbon. And, though a bit time-consuming, it was quite simple to reconstruct her letters from the ribbon."

Derek nodded slowly. "All right. Why were you following her the night her apartment was destroyed?"

"Another lapse of security on Civatech's part,"

Alexi explained. "They may sweep their restricted sections for electronic devices, but they apparently ignore the people who work in the unrestricted sections. During one of my . . . visits to Miss Brown's desk, I scattered a few bugs. Just on the off chance, you understand. Several bugs were planted inside ballpoint pens she used. On the day she voiced her misgivings to her supervisor, she was carrying one of the pens."

Shannon felt a chill. It was unsettling, deeply and coldly unsettling, to know she had been under observation, had been watched and listened to when she had been completely unaware of it. It made her skin crawl.

"Did you figure her for a weak link?" Derek asked impersonally. "Or a target?"

"Given her background, it seemed entirely possible she was an agent. The assumed name, and the connections necessary to place her in a company like Civatech appeared suspect. However, her somewhat naive approach to her supervisor made that theory unlikely. Given her identity, it was also unlikely that she could be turned, and she didn't seem to know enough to be of substantial help to us. But I thought it possible they might move against her; Moreton is known to be paranoid in the extreme at times. Any movement would have been welcome at that point, so I followed her."

Shannon could hardly breathe. She stared fixedly at the floor of the gazebo, risking only a quick glance at Derek's face and finding it unchanged. Had he understood? She felt her skin crawl again at the realization that her background had been checked, her past explored by Alexi. And

Derek would know now that she *had* lied to him about who she was. He had understood Alexi's words, of course he had.

But he didn't comment. He merely said, "All right, Alexi. So what's your objective?"

Alexi smiled faintly. "My *orders* are to locate Cyrano, and take it back with me. It's a prototype; the blueprints were destroyed before Moreton could step in to protect them. To duplicate the device would take years, perhaps decades. It was a joint effort between several technicians, none of whom knew of the overall project. With the device, duplication would be possible—without it, there is no chance."

Derek was smiling. "*Your* objective, Alexi," he said softly.

The other man was smiling as well. "My only concern is that our fanatical Middle Eastern friend not get his hands on such a dangerous weapon. And I don't believe that the balance of power need be upset by anyone else having it. What about your objective, Derek?"

"I want it destroyed. At the very least, defanged."

"Then we're in agreement."

Derek nodded. "I'd say so. A common goal. And we have to move fast. If their attempts to get Shannon are any indication, somebody is panicked and pushing hard. Moreton, I'd guess. Any idea why?"

"A good one, I believe. Word reached us last night that our fanatical friend had attempted to send one of his tankers into U.S. waters flying a neutral flag. Needless to say, the ship was halted and turned back. If that vessel was the intended means to get Cyrano out of the country, Moreton and his partners could be facing a delay that could cost them dearly—especially with Miss Brown, the possessor of troublesome knowledge, on the loose."

"Makes sense." Derek gazed broodingly off into the distance for a moment. Almost absently, he asked, "Any idea who Moreton's partners are?"

"None. But I believe he has at least one, and possibly several. Moreton hasn't the international connections necessary to establish contact in the Middle East. His partners must have that, but they're well-hidden."

After a moment, Derek said, "We'll have to go in. Or else trick Moreton somehow into bringing the device to us."

Alexi appeared mildly interested. "I would like to know, my friend, how you propose to do that."

Derek grinned. "Beats the hell out of me. But, according to everything I've been able to find out, despite Civatech's occasional security lapses that place is the next thing to impregnable. And they'll be nervous, on guard. We don't have a way in. So we'll have to *make* a way out for Cyrano."

"An interesting problem," Alexi murmured.

"That's one way of looking at it." Derek glanced at his watch, then, frowning slightly, looked around at the placid lake and the quiet park.

"What?" Alexi asked quietly.

With a brief grimace, Derek said, "They found us this morning. Too quickly."

Alexi glanced at Shannon, then said, "The Sherlock Holmes maxim. Eliminate the impossible. Whatever remains, no matter how improbable, must be truth."

Derek, too, glanced at Shannon, an odd glance out of shuttered eyes. Then he said softly, "I've done that. I don't like what I'm left with." He shook off the thought almost visibly. "We've no more than a few days, I think. They should have a backup plan for shipment of the device, so they'll move quickly. We have to prevent that—or take advantage of it."

Alexi nodded. "I may be able to discover something."

"We'll meet again later today, then. Here." He sighed and got to his feet, still holding Shannon's hand and pulling her up gently. "Six o'clock."

Alexi agreed with a nod. His gaze flicked to their clasped hands, and he smiled.

"Give my regards to Gina," Derek told him.

"I will."

Seven

Shannon walked quietly at Derek's side as they left the gazebo and went back through the park to his car. One of his cars. She was aware, during that short walk, that he was alert, wary, that his senses probed the areas all around them.

And she felt . . . what did she feel? Disturbed by the meeting with Alexi. For several reasons. Because Alexi knew who she was. Because she understood a little better now, the world both men lived in. A world of danger and deception, a world where some choices meant terrible things. A world where an "enemy" agent could speak casually of plotting an innocent meeting between an unsuspecting woman and another enemy agent.

It was insane! Agents and fanatical Middle Eastern men bent on taking over the world, dangerous devices, hired killers, and secret meetings. She was so *ordinary*: things like this just didn't happen to ordinary people.

"Shannon?"

She realized they were standing by the car, and she hastily got in the passenger side. Her hand felt cold now without his holding it, and she felt alone. *You're turning into a clinging vine, Shannon! You'd better get used to being alone; he won't always be here. He may not be here for much longer . . .* Or she wouldn't be. She'd run, like she always had.

Run . . . run . . . run . . . It echoed in her mind, a mocking litany of failure. And with it were other echoes, rebounding in her head jarringly. *"I care about you."* But had he made love to Gina? *"You must have looked very much like a white knight to her . . ."* Yes, she could believe that . . . easily, because that was what he had been to her. *Lover.* But just for one night! Wasn't she allowed just one night? She wasn't cherishing any illusions, she didn't think he was hers forever.

Did she?

The homey little burrow welcomed them with its undisturbed silence. Derek hadn't said anything at all during the ride, and neither had Shannon. She caught herself limping as she went into the living room, and hastily sat down on the couch, swearing inwardly. Always giving away her insecurities.

Quickly, she asked, "What were you and Alexi talking about at first? That about the sun setting in the west? And something about an end run?"

Derek moved to look out the front window. "Alexi's coming over to our side for good—that's what he meant about the sun setting in the west. And an end run is a football play and military tactic where the aggressor runs wide around his own left or right flank while they block for him. In other words, Alexi is letting his people think he's over here doing their work, while he fully intends to *stay* here. Rather than an open and dramatic defection, he's just slipping away from them."

"Oh. I see."

"Shannon?" Derek sat down in a chair beside the couch and lit a cigarette. "You haven't said a word about letting your mother know you're all right."

She started. "Oh. Well, she's—she wouldn't have heard about the explosion."

"Why not?" Derek asked mildly.

"She's . . . out of the country."

Derek blew a smoke ring and studied it critically. In the same mild tone, he asked, "Don't you think it's time you told me who you really are, Shannon?"

She opened her mouth to answer that he knew who she was, that she'd told him, but a sudden thought made her go cold all over. What was it Alexi had said? Derek obviously had been bothered by the fact that they had been found so quickly at the loft, and Alexi had said something about eliminating the impossible . . . and then they'd both looked at her so oddly.

"I didn't," she whispered.

He looked at her, frowning. "You didn't what?"

"Tell them. I didn't tell them where we were. You were with me all the time, you know I didn't use the phone, or—"

He was suddenly beside her on the couch, the cigarette stubbed out in an ashtray on the coffee table. Suddenly beside her and his expression was grave. "I know you didn't, sweetheart." One of his arms lay along the back of the couch behind her; his free hand covered both of hers where they twisted together in her lap.

She stared down at his hand, and a laugh emerged shakily. "That would have been devious, wouldn't it? If I had come to you pretending to ask for your help, but really just trying to lead someone else to you—"

"Stop it, Shannon." His hand tightened around hers. "Stop expecting to be blamed for what happens. None of this has been your fault." After a moment, he added softly, "Now, why don't you tell me who you are so it won't worry you anymore?"

She sent him a quick glance. "It doesn't worry you?"

He smiled. "No. Based on what Alexi said, I can guess. He didn't know about Governor Franklin's influence, but he knew somebody had pulled strings to get you into Civatech. He also knew that Brown was an assumed name, and yet you had security clearance at the company. And he believed that, because of who you really are, it wouldn't have been likely that you could be turned traitor. So, when he looked into your background, he found a great deal of political power and/or wealth."

Shannon was gazing at him in fascination. "Um . . . both," she murmured.

Derek nodded, unsurprised. "And I can also guess that you broke completely with your family, to the point of taking a different name and struggling to make it on your own without any help from them."

She took a deep breath. "My mother and stepfather live in a very high-powered world. I didn't fit.

And my mother just couldn't understand that. It seemed to her I wasn't trying hard enough. But I did," she added softly.

He waited quietly, watching her delicate face, thinking how wrong and dangerous it was to force a fragile spirit into an unyielding mold.

In the same soft voice, she went on. "My father —my real father—was a diplomat. He died when . . . he died in the crash. My mother wasn't in the car. A few years later, my mother married Marshall Burke. You've probably heard of him."

Derek had. The Burkes had been political and financial powers in the world for a long time. Marshall Burke, Derek remembered, was now the U.S. ambassador to the United Nations. And no wonder Alexi had come to the conclusion that Shannon would hardly turn traitor; her background was filled with the kind of wealth that made treason highly unlikely and political realities that made it virtually impossible.

"Did Burke adopt you?" he asked.

She nodded. "So my real name is Burke. I . . . I'm sorry I lied to you, Derek. I just didn't want—"

"I know." He smiled at her. "And now that it's out in the open, you don't have to worry about it anymore. I suppose William knows who you really are?"

Shannon bit her lip. "No. When he got me the job at Civatech, he vouched for me; there wasn't a security check. He thought I didn't want them to find out about—about being arrested that time."

"I see." Derek's smile went a bit crooked. "Now will you please relax and believe that I never, for one moment, suspected you of being on the other side?"

She managed a smile. "If you say so."

"I do." He leaned over suddenly and kissed her.

The movement was so quick, the kiss so brief, that Shannon didn't have time to stiffen. She just looked at him, uneasy at this reminder of what else lay between them.

But Derek was still casual, his calm voice belying the heat in his dark eyes. "Definitely those big eyes. It doesn't seem to matter what you're wearing."

She blinked, remembering. And as color rose in her cheeks, she tried to change the subject. "Um . . . how do you think they'll get Cyrano out of the country?"

"On the tanker," he murmured, smiling a little.

Shannon was trying to think clearly. "But he—Alexi—said the tanker had been turned back."

Derek nodded, but not as if his mind were completely on the subject of tankers. "Sure. But it won't go far. Outside U.S. waters, it'll wait."

"Wait for what?"

"For Civatech's ship."

Shannon felt bewildered, and knew it was largely because of those warm eyes fixed on her so intently. She was finding it almost impossible to think clearly. "Civatech's ship . . . oh, I remember now. They do have a ship to transport up and down the East Coast. But if that's the case, why do they need the tanker at all?"

"To transport Cyrano to the Middle East. Civatech's ship won't go near the place—it would look too suspicious to our military ships out there. No, they'll transfer the device at sea, far from watching eyes."

She cleared her throat. Why did he keep looking at her like that? She felt hot. "So their backup plan in case the tanker couldn't reach port was to use their own ship innocently? You said it would only be days—"

"You're still on the loose," Derek reminded her. "I'm betting they were pretty confident that the tanker could reach port. Since it couldn't, they'll make use of one of their regular shipments out of—Norfolk, I believe. I don't know the schedule, but Civatech ships their stuff out pretty regularly. They can't afford to look suspicious by shipping out early, so they'll stick to their schedule."

"How can we find out when the ship will leave?"

"That's the easy part," Derek said dryly.

Shannon thought about it. *Tried* to think about it. "Um . . . then the hard part is getting Cyrano?"

His gaze was moving over her face slowly, as if he were memorizing her features, and the look alone was a caress. "They can't afford to use unusual security," he murmured. "It has to be a regular shipment, overland, to Norfolk. Probably in a semi, or a big van of some kind."

Shannon pulled air into her lungs slowly, wondering when she'd last breathed. A minute? An hour? "You said—there would have to be a trick of some kind to get Cyrano out?"

Derek shook his head, still obviously somewhat detached from the subject. "To get Cyrano in our hands. I thought about it on the way back here. If they were transporting the device secretly and surrounding it with security, they wouldn't have panicked and moved against you so fast—there wouldn't have been a need for that. They feel vulnerable. That means their plan is wide open to possible interference."

"So what do we do?" Such a small room, really,

filled with his presence. She looked down at the hand covering hers and fought a sudden wild urge to throw herself into his arms.

"First, we find out when the next shipment leaves Civatech. It'll have to be the next; that tanker can't hang around outside U.S. waters for long without being challenged." He drew a deep breath. "Shannon—"

The doorbell rang.

Shannon jumped, startled, only dimly aware that the bell rang with an odd rhythm, as if the visitor were deliberately using the bell as a signal. And obviously she was correct about the signal, because after a fleeting moment of tension, Derek relaxed and rose from the couch with a frown.

"Now, what the hell—" he muttered, going to the front door with the confidence of a man who knows only too well what's on the other side.

Shannon couldn't see the door, but gazed toward the foyer, half relieved and half annoyed by the interruption. What had he been about to say to her?

"I just put two and two together, that's all," Raven Long said as she strolled into the living room, looking, just like last time, as if she could have fit into any situation. "Hello, Shannon. It wasn't that I knew where to look, Derek, it was just that I knew *how* to look. Shannon, this is my husband, Josh. And a friend of ours, Zach Steele."

Shannon looked at the two men. One was dark, lean, and curiously both elegant and tough in his casual clothes; the other was equally dark, massive and dangerous and graceful. Josh Long possessed a handsomeness that was a bit hawklike, his blue eyes penetrating and intelligent. He was,

Shannon thought, a man who would make a very good friend and a dangerous enemy. And Zach Steele was a large man of obvious physical strength who, like Derek, handled both his size and undoubted power with a casual grace that was riveting.

She gazed at them as the three visitors settled casually into chairs, and she felt distinctly unnerved until Derek returned to her side and took her hand.

"Out with it," he said, directing the command to Raven. "I want to know how you found us."

"You forget." She smiled merrily. "Unlike your enemies, I know all about your lurid past. It wasn't very hard to track down your attorney in New York and—um—persuade him to tell us what properties you owned here in Richmond, whether your name was on the deeds or not."

Derek stared at her for a moment, and then eyed Josh Long somewhat severely. "You leaned on him, dammit."

Josh, lighting a cigarette, sent Derek a bland look over the flame of his lighter. "Nice to have clout," he murmured.

Wincing slightly, Derek said, "I knew that comment would come back to haunt me." He gave Raven a painful look.

Unrepentant, she shrugged. "Josh had already figured out that you weren't a garden-variety agent, pal. I just filled in a few of the blanks for him."

"Fill them in for me," Shannon said suddenly, her earlier unrest disappearing.

Raven looked at Derek with lifted brows, and he sighed as he turned his gaze to Shannon. "It isn't important. They just mean that I inherited, through an accident of birth, a company that makes me—financially independent."

In a polite tone, Josh said, "One might put it that way."

Shannon understood the burrows now, and the cars and elaborate security systems. It didn't really surprise her to learn that Derek was a wealthy man, but she didn't know how she felt about it. It didn't seem to matter.

Derek looked back at the visitors and changed the subject in a firm voice. "Now that we've gotten that out of the way, and now that we know *how* you found us—what are you doing here?"

Injured, Raven said, "Helping, of course."

"I told you—"

"I hate being told what to do," Josh said conversationally, glancing at Zach. "Don't you?"

"Always." The big man's voice was soft, his serene gray eyes amused.

"All right, all right," Derek said. "You're here."

"Graceful acceptance," Josh said, again to Zach.

Derek grinned suddenly. "I'd love to go head-to-head with you in a boardroom."

"I'd love to watch," Raven murmured. "From a concrete bunker."

"Now that we've gotten *that* out of the way," Zach said.

Shannon understood what was going on, which surprised her somewhat. There was, she thought, something interesting between Derek and Josh Long. Two powerful and wealthy men, both accustomed to command, both tough. She had the odd feeling that, although neither wished for a confrontation, a test of strength, both wondered how the contest would turn out. Like Raven, Shannon would have been a fascinated observer should it ever come to pass and, like Raven, she'd opt for the safety of a bunker.

"I gather you people have been investigating?" Derek said now, briskly, to the visitors.

"We've been doing our poor best," Josh replied.

Zach cleared his throat and spoke rather quickly. "We have Civatech's transport schedule to Norfolk, and their ship leaves port day after tomorrow for a regular shipment."

Derek used his free hand to fumble for a cigarette and light it, his expression thoughtful. "When is the next transport to Norfolk?"

"Tomorrow afternoon. The scheduled route is just over a hundred and twenty-five miles long. They usually use two trucks, vans rather than semis. The stuff will be inspected by customs before they load it on the ship."

"Does that help?" Raven asked.

Nodding slowly, Derek said, "Definitely. It's what I needed to know." He looked at Zach. "I had it in mind to destroy this device, but it's supposed to be practically indestructible. Tell me—how long would it take you to disarm this thing and wipe the programming?"

Zach considered for a moment. "Well, without knowing exactly what I'd be dealing with, it's hard to say. Any idea how it's armed?"

"From what I've been able to find out, lasers. It also has the capability to launch small armor-piercing missiles. God knows what else it's capable of."

Shrugging, Zach said, "The lasers will be simple. As to the programming, the more complicated they make it, the easier it is to throw a spanner in the works. Say two or three hours. Less if it's partially disassembled."

"It's a prototype?" Josh asked.

Derek nodded. "No blueprints or diagrams exist. If we gum up the works badly enough, it'll be useless to them. And useless is the name of the game."

"Lot easier to break something than fix it," Zach noted.

Shannon listened intently to the ensuing discussion. Clearly, Derek had accepted the help of Raven and the two men. Just as clearly, these three people were as accustomed to deceptions and tactics as Derek.

Diagrams were carefully drawn, maps poured over, and a route marked. Shannon was asked to describe the trucks Civatech used, and was able to remember them clearly. She became interested in spite of herself, fascinated by the intricacies of the plan that gradually evolved.

Zach went out to get something for lunch when they realized it was midafternoon, and it wasn't until they were eating in the kitchen that Raven dryly asked the questions lurking in Shannon's mind.

"So how are you going to know which truck the device is in?" she asked Derek. "And who stops the other one?"

Derek was silent for a moment. "The other truck will be diverted by some friends of mine," he said slowly. "I think they'd rather none of you saw them, or knew any more than necessary about them."

Alexi, Shannon thought. *And Gina.*

Raven nodded, as unquestioning and incurious as her husband and their friend, accepting matter-of-factly Derek's implied trust in these "friends" of his. "Okay. What about the decision of which truck *we* stop?"

Derek hesitated again. He was frowning slightly, his gaze distracted for a moment, and then he returned Raven's steady look with a faint smile. "I'll know."

She nodded, accepting that as well without question.

Shannon put it together in her mind. Alexi and his partner would divert the other truck, delaying it long enough so that both would arrive in Norfolk at about the same time. While that diversion was taking place, the truck they were interested in would be stopped so that Zach could "defang" Cyrano. With that done, Zach would assume the place of the driver and deliver the shipment to Norfolk where, according to what Josh had discovered, Adam Moreton waited on Civatech's ship.

Zach had more or less commandeered the job of delivering the truck to Norfolk, saying merely that Derek would want to remain in Richmond. And, after a steady look at the other man and a thoughtful silence, Derek had agreed.

So he can take care of me, Shannon thought. And she didn't know how she felt about that. She couldn't seem to feel at all, except for surface emotions.

"It's a tight timetable," Zach noted.

Derek nodded. "Tighter than you know. There's another player in the game, Moreton's silent partner. Or partners. This shell game may bring him out into the open, but I'm gambling he won't show up in time."

Raven tilted her head questioningly. "He's the danger to Shannon, then?"

"I think so. Until Cyrano is safely aboard Yaltan's ship. After that, the whole thing'll probably break wide open. Civatech's ship will sail with the morning tide on Friday, and Moreton will want best speed to meet Yaltan's tanker as soon as possible."

"What will happen to Moreton?" Shannon asked suddenly.

Derek met her gaze steadily. "Yaltan won't be happy. He'll be getting a harmless, useless device instead of the killing machine he expects."

She took a deep breath. Yaltan, the Middle Eastern fanatic Alexi had described who wanted to conquer the world. "He'll kill Moreton?"

"Probably," Raven answered. Her voice was flat. "But he was willing to sell his soul and upset the balance of power, Shannon. He was willing to kill millions."

Shannon pushed her salad away. Choices. Derek's plan would send Adam Moreton to a probable death. She thought of the brisk, somewhat impatient, middle-aged Moreton; he didn't *look* like an evil man.

"They tried to kill you," Derek reminded her.

She looked at him, at that hard, handsome face with its ancient dark eyes. She thought she understood, now, why his eyes were old and tolerant. How many impossible choices had he made?

"You said something about an appointment this afternoon." Raven's voice was easy and casual.

Derek looked away from Shannon with obvious reluctance. "Yes. I have to meet that friend of mine. And there's something else I need to do before our game plan will work."

Raven glanced at her husband, then said, "Why don't Josh and I stay with Shannon while you're gone?"

"And I," Zach said placidly, "will wait in the car while you meet your friend."

Derek looked at each of the visitors in turn, an expression of faint amusement on his face. "You had this all planned, huh?"

His ex-partner smiled at him. "Of course not."

"All right, dammit," Derek said and sighed. He rose from the kitchen table and gently pulled Shannon to her feet. "We'll leave in a couple of minutes, Zach."

"Right." The big security expert headed for the garage, while Raven and Josh began clearing the dishes.

Puzzled, Shannon followed Derek into the living room. "What do you have to do?" she whispered.

He shook his head a bit as he stood looking down at her. "I'll tell you later. Do you mind staying here with Raven and Josh, honey?"

"No." She felt vaguely uneasy. "No, of course not."

Derek's hands lifted to hold her shoulders gently, and he bent his head suddenly to kiss her. It wasn't a light kiss, and there was nothing at all casual about it. It was hungry, urgent, and more: There was something else, something Shannon sensed but couldn't define.

But her body didn't care. She melted against him, forgetting all her reservations, forgetting that she had rationally decided this explosion between them had to be defused. Nothing mattered except the radiant warmth of him, the desire in his kiss, the urgency of his body.

And when the devastating kiss finally ended, she could only stare up at him dazedly. "Derek—"

He touched her cheek lightly with his fingertips, his dark eyes hot and restless. Then, abruptly and in a grating voice, he said, "I love you, Shannon." And he was gone.

She sat down in the chair behind her, hardly aware of moving. Dimly, she heard the grinding sound of the garage door opening, heard the car start. The distant noises faded, and she sat feeling more shaken than ever before in her life.

"I love you, Shannon."

She looked up as Raven and Josh returned to the living room. "What did he have to do?" she asked softly.

Raven looked at her for a moment, as if weighing something. "There are still a couple of wild cards in the game, Shannon. Those two assassins. They have to be put out of commission."

"How?" The question was unnaturally calm.

Josh lit a cigarette and expelled smoke in a brief, hard burst. "Any way possible," he said bluntly.

The remainder of the afternoon and evening dragged on. Shannon was grateful to her companions, who were casual but friendly, and made it possible for her to be the same. And she envied them their love; it was obvious in every glance, something deep and utterly certain.

It must be a wonderful feeling, she thought, that certainty. To be certain of each other. To be certain of love.

Shannon's own unleashed emotions were turbulent. She felt as if some giant whirlpool had caught her, snatched her from a calm sea, and carried her inexorably in dizzying circles toward— something. And she was afraid.

Love? He loved her? No. No, that wasn't possible. Men like Derek didn't love women like her. She believed in his desire only because it was impossible to deny. But, love?

The hours passed, and she talked to her companions with surface calm. When it grew late, she yielded to Raven's gentle suggestion and took a shower before sliding into bed. In her room. Derek had rather pointedly put their bags in two different rooms this morning after she had . . .

After you told him it had all happened too fast.

Shannon lay in the big, lonely bed and stared at a dark ceiling. But it had happened too fast, she assured hrself. And he was a man outside her experience.

A good thing, too, or you'd be dead.

She tried to ignore the little voice in her head, but it was impossible. There was no one, she acknowledged, she could have gone to who would have been better for her that first night than Derek. He had, without hesitation and apparently without feeling it a burden, simply begun taking care of her.

And, not content with merely protecting her from a threat against her life, Derek had also insisted, gently but firmly, that she accept herself, that she stop thinking of her flaw. He had asked for her trust, openly, had moved closer and closer to her until she couldn't back away from him, couldn't withdraw. He had never attempted to hide himself from her. He had tried to protect her even in the face of the explosive passion between them, had tried to give her the room and the time she needed.

But there hadn't been time. There wasn't time now. And this caring man with the old eyes, this man who made impossibly tough choices and decisions without apology, this man who had taught her to feel shattering desire . . . this incredible man had said that he loved her.

And now he was out there, somewhere, putting two hired killers out of commission—any way he could.

Shannon felt cold. She rubbed her silk-clad arms beneath the covers absently, all her senses straining, hearing only the low voices of Raven and Josh Long in the living room. The coldness was numbing. Derek's absence brought home to her just how much she'd grown to depend on him . . . in every way.

But he won't always be here.

Was that it? Was she so certain of being alone again soon that she was trying to protect a part of herself from that pain? Was that why her feelings seemed muffled, oddly distant?

Shannon stiffened suddenly, hearing a door open, hearing two more voices added to the murmurs in the living room. She lay gazing up at the ceiling, her heart pounding, aware of a profound relief that wasn't distant at all.

After a few minutes, the voices died with the closing of a door, and there was silence. She turned her head to stare at the open doorway of the bedroom, and within a moment, Derek's large, powerful silhouette appeared.

"Shannon?"

"I'm glad you're back," she said steadily.

It seemed for an instant as though Derek would have come into her room; he took a step inside the doorway, then hesitated and moved back out into the hall. "Good night, honey," he said.

She couldn't see his face. "Good night."

Shannon knew he wouldn't force the issue. He wouldn't slide into her bed in the middle of the night. He wouldn't demand a vow of love from her in return for his own.

She closed her eyes, trying to relax. But she couldn't. Her body was tense, restless. She was cold. It would be over soon, really over. She'd have to start all over again with her life. That, curiously enough, didn't frighten her. The thought of a new job, a new apartment, was just a matter-of-fact realization in her mind.

Shannon was sitting up before she realized, sliding to the edge of the bed, throwing the covers back. She paused there for a moment, trying to think.

He wouldn't come to her. He said he loved her, but he wouldn't pressure her. He wouldn't make love to her again unless she went to him, unless she chose consciously to forget her own determination to have more time.

Would time really make a difference?

Eight

Derek wanted to sleep, and he certainly needed to. Unfortunately, he had found that his own weariness had little effect on either his body or his worried thoughts. He couldn't stop thinking. He was losing Shannon, he felt that like a cold lead weight in the pit of his belly. Too much had happened too fast for her.

He couldn't blame her for that. Couldn't blame her for wanting to just get away from all of it—including him. She hadn't said it, but he knew that was what she wanted.

He couldn't be rational about it, even though he tried. It was no good understanding that she *needed* time, that he should just back off for a while. He was simply afraid that the bond between them was too fragile, that, once away from him, she'd be lost to him for good.

She had come alive in his arms last night, caught up in the wildness of passion between them. If they had not been torn so abruptly from their bed, perhaps . . . but they had. And the situation around them, so foreign and threatening to her, only compounded her uncertainties.

If only—

"Derek?"

He sat up quickly, looking across the darkened room, suddenly aware of his heartbeat because he could feel it throughout his entire body. Her silk pajamas caught the faint light as she crossed the room to the bed, and he was afraid to move when her slight weight settled beside him.

"Those two men—what happened?" she asked softly.

Derek cleared his throat. "They're being held by a couple of Zach's security men. They'll be turned over to the police."

"Then it will be over, won't it?"

"Most of it," he said steadily. "But *we* won't be over, Shannon. I don't want to lose you. I love you."

Still in the same soft, distant voice, she said, "It's an illusion, you know. They do it with mirrors and lights."

He felt his jaw aching, realizing only then that his jaw was clenched. "And what about what happened between us last night? Was that an illusion?"

"No." She hesitated. "I never wanted to need anybody. I never did. But I need you, Derek. I don't seem to have much of a choice about it."

Derek reached out slowly and touched her face, aching inside at the reluctance in her voice. It wasn't what he wanted to hear, that reluctance. But at least she admitted need, and that was something to build on. He hoped. "Honey . . ."

She came into his arms instantly, naturally, no hesitation or reluctance in that. "Make love to me," she whispered against his throat. "You make me forget, and I want to forget." She lifted her face for his kiss, and a sound of stark need tangled in the back of her throat as the kiss detonated desire.

It swept over them even more powerfully than before, carrying them both in a surging tidal wave, an unstoppable force. As if the memory of that brutal interruption of before haunted them both, they were frantic, driven. There wasn't enough time, there could never be enough time for them. They were greedy, their bodies ravenous for each other.

And when that shattering wave crested and Derek hoarsely whispered his love for her, Shannon held him and cried out wildly. But not of love, never of love, because she couldn't love him. She *couldn't*.

In the peaceful aftermath, Shannon was troubled by a niggling question, and even as she reminded herself silently that she didn't have the right to ask, she heard her voice emerge. "Did you see Gina tonight?"

Derek shifted a bit to pull her even closer. "No. I just talked to Alexi." His voice, like hers, was hushed. After a moment, he added, "We were never lovers, Shannon."

She wondered if he could read her mind, or if her jealousy was so obvious. Jealousy? No, not that, of course. "It's none of my business," she whispered.

"Yes, it is," he told her. "You have the right to

ask any question you want and expect an honest answer."

Shannon was silent, not agreeing or disagreeing. But his statement left her free to ask something she had wondered about, and she wasn't sure how to phrase the question. Even in the frantic necessity of their passion, Derek hadn't forgotten to take precautions, and she wasn't sure whether to be warmed or appalled by the fact that, in equipping all his burrows, he had apparently thought of everything.

"What is it?" he asked softly, aware of her slight tension.

She thought about it, discovering somewhat to her surprise that the darkness did indeed make her feel different—at least when she was with him. The question wasn't as hard to ask as she'd expected it to be.

"Um . . . did you plan to have a woman hiding out with you in your burrows?"

There was a moment of silence, and the Derek chuckled. "Hardly. But the kind of training I've had teaches you to be prepared for anything, and I believe in being responsible for my actions."

It was, she thought, a very important part of this man. And she didn't believe another kind of man could have lived the life Derek had lived. The simple truth was that he was too much a caregiver and too responsible a man to allow anyone else to make the tough decisions for him.

"Shannon?"

"Hmmm?"

"I love you."

She burrowed closer, silent, aware of hot tears dammed behind her closed eyelids. He'd gotten close, but not that close. She couldn't let him get that close. When this was over and he was gone, there had to be a part of her he hadn't touched. There *had* to be. She wouldn't survive otherwise.

Derek lay awake long after she breathed evenly in relaxed sleep, holding her and staring up at the ceiling. Pushing. He was pushing, and he knew it. He could feel her slip away from him in some elusive fashion he couldn't even name. And he was so afraid she'd slip away for good.

She came to him in the night out of need, but when her world was back to normal would she still need him?

"They aren't being very bright about this," Raven said consideringly. "Sending two trucks out an hour apart is just inviting trouble. At least if they were together, one couldn't be stopped without the other driver noticing."

"Lucky for us it's this way," Shannon murmured.

They were standing together on the edge of a clearing a good twenty-five yards away from the main road, waiting for Derek, Josh, and Zach to rejoin them. The men were keeping watch over Civatech's entrance and waiting for the first truck to depart on schedule.

Behind Shannon and Raven, looking peculiarly ungainly as it waited silently out of its natural habitat, sat a helicopter. The plan called for Josh to pilot the craft several miles along the expected route of the trucks, where they intended to divert the truck containing Cyrano and stop it.

Shannon, thinking about the fact that only she and Derek were unarmed, said slowly, "He really doesn't use guns?"

Raven smiled. "He really doesn't. With Derek, it's almost an abhorrence. If you ever see him use a gun, it'll be because the situation is so desperate, and the outcome so important to him, that he's putting aside the beliefs of a lifetime."

Shannon looked at her searchingly. "You know him very well, don't you?"

"Not as well as you do," Raven replied calmly.

Startled, Shannon said, "You've known him so much longer, worked with him—"

"I haven't been in love with him."

Shannon moved jerkily in unconscious denial. But Raven spoke before she could.

"It's tough when your world is knocked off balance by a situation—or a man." She was gazing at nothing, her expression abstracted. "Worse when it's both. And when the situation is larger than life, something right out of a suspense novel or a James Bond movie, it's easy to believe nothing's real." She looked at Shannon suddenly, her lovely face intense. "But don't let yourself be fooled by that, Shannon. Because it's in a situation like this that *everything* is real."

"What do you mean?" Shannon asked, her voice little more than a whisper.

Raven hesitated, then spoke in a tone that needed no dramatics to be emphatic; the words were enough. "Shannon, from the moment your apartment blew up in front of you, you were thrown into a world where everything's black or white. Everything. Truth or lie. There are no shades of gray in this world. Not in *this* world.

"Don't think about the life you've known in twenty-some-odd years. Don't think about the roles people play, the games they play, or the ways they pretend when a man and a woman get involved with each other. There's no room here for that. The civilized layers get stripped away, and the only thing left is truth—and instinct. Because tomorrow we *really* may die."

Shannon felt cold, but forced a small laugh. "But this isn't the normal world. It isn't my world."

"It is now," Raven told her. "You can't go back, not completely. Shannon, you'll have a foot in this world for the rest of your life, because you've seen the reality of it. And that isn't necessarily a bad thing; because of these last few days, you'll cherish all the future ones. And you'll realize that what you feel is truth, because there's no time for lies."

"What if—what if I don't know what I feel?"

"Trust your instincts. There are moments when you have to make choices, especially in this world. And it's in those moments when your instincts will tell you the truth. Just listen to them."

A silence fell between them, and Shannon brooded over what the other woman had said.

She had slipped out of bed early this morning while Derek slept, and he had found her almost an hour later cooking breakfast. He had said nothing about their night together, and neither had Shannon. It was afternoon now, and the hours since breakfast had been busily filled with preparations, with phone calls to arrange things, and conferences with their confederates, and all the other details of a plan.

They hadn't really talked.

Shannon was acutely aware of her own lack of response when Derek had said he loved her. Three times, he had said it to her with calm and utter certainty, not in the heat of passion. The first time, he'd been gone too quickly for her to respond. The second time, she had called love a trick of mirrors and lights. The third time, she had said nothing at all.

She had believed this strange new world was a thing of illusion, of deception, yet Raven said it was—the ultimate reality. And as she thought about it, Shannon slowly began to agree. Hadn't she been conscious all along that time was something snatched, stolen from events? Hadn't she felt smothered by the sensation of too little time with too much happening?

It was so different from the life she was accustomed to, where time dragged and emotions maintained a steady balance between uncomfortable and puzzling extremes. Now every moment was sharply etched, every emotion poignant. Was this what so many people searched for in vain, this heightened awareness of time and events and emotions?

Had she in fact stumbled into a world more real than anything since man was young, a place where civilization blunted nothing because this world existed on the sharp edge of what was primitive and real?

And if that were true, why were her own instincts telling her nothing? She didn't know if she believed that Derek loved her. She didn't know how she felt herself, because there was something inside her she was afraid to see, something distant and protected. And she was still afraid nothing was *real.*

Not real . . . and almost over.

• • •

"There it is." Derek raised the binoculars and focused on the unmarked van pulling out of Civatech's shipping area. He watched it as the vehicle reached the main road and headed east, and Josh, watching him, saw him tense slightly. After a moment, Derek laid aside the binoculars and reached for the walkie-talkie that was beside him on the ground. "That's ours."

"How can you tell?" Zach asked.

Derek hesitated, then said, "I recognize the driver." He pressed the send button on the walkie-talkie and spoke softly. "Alexi."

"Go," a voice whispered back.

"The second truck is yours. Good luck."

"Same to you. See you in the want ads."

Derek chuckled as he picked up the binoculars and rose to his feet, and as Josh and Zach rose also, the former asked a polite question.

"Want ads?"

"Where else would you expect to find two out-of-work spies?" Derek asked reasonably.

Josh thought that over as they headed back into the woods to join the two women. "Alexi," he murmured. "Could be a Russian name, I suppose. Possible. And on our side, too. Just making an educated guess based on the fact that he's wearing a white hat at the moment, I'd say he's going to be running his ad in U.S. papers."

"Good guess," Derek said.

Glancing aside at Zach, Josh said dryly, "This guy could give you a contest when it comes to clams."

Derek chuckled again. "You didn't ask me anything."

"All right. Is the second out-of-work spy yourself?"

"That depends on Shannon," Derek said lightly. "If she gives me my walking papers, I may well join the Foreign Legion. If not, I think I'll dust off my seat in the boardroom."

The other two men might have replied, but they didn't get the chance. The clearing where the women and a helicopter waited came into view, and they were greeted by Raven's pained voice.

"They also serve who only stand and wait. . . ."

"Well, why didn't you warm up the bird?" Josh asked severely, taking her hand and leading her toward it. "That would have been useful."

"Because the *last* time I did," she reminded him, "you nearly had a heart attack when I took off accidentally."

Josh shuddered at the memory. "True."

Derek reached out to take Shannon's hand as they neared the helicopter, looking down at her intently. "All right?" he asked softly.

She nodded. "Fine." She really didn't know how else to answer him.

Derek squeezed her hand, but said nothing else as they climbed into the helicopter. Josh and Zach conferred via headsets in the front, Josh piloting while his friend navigated, and it took less than an hour for them to reach the spot where they planned to waylay the Civatech truck.

It was a lonely stretch of road, little traveled, and conveniently full of potholes. Shannon watched in fascination as huge pieces of machinery were brought out of the woods where they'd been secreted this morning. Road signs were set up and various tools placed prominently. Hard hats and yellow vests transformed all five of them into workers.

"Although," Zach said, eyeing the women thoughtfully, "I've never seen anything like you two on a road gang."

"Chauvinist," Raven accused absently, tucking her long black hair underneath her hard hat.

"What if a state trooper comes by?" Shannon asked, coping with her own hair.

"We have all the necessary papers," Derek told her as he stood back to study their diversion. "That's got it, I think. We should look busy, but not *too* busy. We don't want anybody getting suspicious." He checked his watch. "We've got maybe an hour before the truck gets here."

Zach started up the engine of an enormous asphalt rolling machine and, after a philosophical shrug and a "might as well" to the rest, began to work on the road. He obviously knew what he was doing.

Shannon stood at one end of their "working" area with a sign advising motorists to either stop or slow down, depending on which way she turned the sign. Raven stood at the other end with an identical sign, while the men drove machinery and waved tools and moved busily between.

Three cars were maneuvered through the partially blocked road before the Civatech truck arrived. And, in the end, it was ridiculously simple. Everyone was keeping an eye out for the truck, so when Shannon stopped it because Zach had the road totally blocked with his machine, Derek and Josh were already moving smoothly to either side of the van.

Derek opened the driver's door and pulled the somewhat large man out as if he weighed nothing, while Josh slid behind the wheel and immediately drove the van off the road, where it was hidden by the trees.

"What the hell—" the driver blustered as his hands were being efficiently cuffed behind his back with regulation police handcuffs.

"Ever heard of a hijacking?" Derek asked politely, herding the man toward the van.

The driver went white. "There's nothing in there! Just a bunch of electronic parts—nothing valuable!"

"That's all right." Derek's voice was soothing. "We don't want much."

Incredibly, within ten minutes the busy clutter of a road crew was gone. Machinery, tools, and signs were returned to the shelter of the woods, along with hard hats and yellow vests. The protesting driver was ordered to sit on the ground by a tree, watched over by a smiling Raven holding a wicked handgun.

"Shannon?" Zach was just inside the van, an opened wooden crate pulled to the doorway. "This it?"

She accepted Derek's hand as she climbed into the van, absently noting that the opened crate was the third Zach had tried. She looked into the crate, and recognized it instantly. "That's it. But it's—"

"In three pieces," Zach said with a grunt of satisfaction. "Much easier for me."

Derek helped Shannon back down from the van, holding her hand firmly once she was beside him on the ground. "How long will it take, Zach?"

"Couple of hours. We want to make damned certain this thing could never be called a weapon—right?"

"Right."

"Okay, then. Say two hours. Josh, hand me that tool bag, will you?"

Derek led Shannon off to the side, until they were out of hearing of the others but still within sight.

"They won't know it's been tampered with?" she asked, needing to say something.

"No. Not, at least, until they put it together and try to make it work. They'll know then."

"We could just throw the crate away somewhere once Cyrano's harmless," she said.

Derek looked at her steadily. "Keep Moreton from delivering a worthless device to Yaltan, you mean?"

"Is it really necessary—"

"You tell me. We could get rid of the device, and Yaltan wouldn't get his hands on Moreton. Then what? Leave Moreton free to sell the next dangerous toy?"

"The police—"

"Yes. The police. We don't have evidence that would stand up in court. There could have been a mix-up in the shipping orders, just like there could have been a mix-up with the order to destroy Cyrano. Yaltan sure as hell wouldn't testify, even if anyone would believe him. So we go to the police, and they have a device that doesn't exist and an upright citizen screaming bloody murder. Maybe the military would step in, but Moreton's probably got a cover story ready for them just in case. We'd be the ones in jail, Shannon."

She drew a deep breath. Choices. Hard choices. "How can you . . . do things like this?"

He searched her delicate face intently, realizing that she wasn't horrified, but bewildered. "Remember what Alexi said? Does the end justify the means—it always comes down to that. I can't answer that question, honey. It's a philosophical question: It can be argued in classrooms, and debated as a political platform, and tossed around on a Sunday afternoon because there's nothing better to do. But it can't be answered in the abstract—only the concrete."

Touching her cheek gently, he said, "I don't want this to happen again, do you understand? I want you safe. I want Yaltan mad as hell so he thinks twice before he accepts another shady deal. I want Moreton out of Civatech because one failure won't make him give up, and I want him punished because this was more than treason. And I want a stake driven through the heart of that electronic monster over there, because it doesn't belong in a sane world."

After a moment, he finished softly, "I do things like this because I can, Shannon. Because this solution makes sense to me. And because I can't *not* do it."

She looked up at him for a long minute, and then slid her arms around his waist and listened to his heart beat beneath her cheek. It was the first time she had reached out spontaneously to him in the light of day, but she didn't think about that. She just thought about strong men with old eyes and caring hearts who made tough choices.

"I'm glad you can't *not* do it," she murmured finally.

Derek hugged her, and then asked, "How's the hip?"

She looked up at him in surprise, and he chuckled softly. "You haven't been limping."

It was true, she realized. With so much to think about, consciousness of her "flaw" had been totally absent. She hadn't even been aware of it when confronted by Raven's stylish beauty and easy confidence. "I—I guess I forgot."

He held her face in both of his big hands and smiled down at her. "You're beautiful, Shannon."

She wanted to look away, but couldn't escape the vibrant warmth of those sapphire-flecked dark eyes. "Thank you. Thank you for everything."

His smile faded a little. "For what? For the truth? Don't thank me for that."

"Then how about for saving my life?" she asked unsteadily.

He hesitated, then said roughly, "You would have saved yourself. You're a survivor, honey. You may not punch life in the nose, but you keep getting up when you're knocked down. In case you hadn't realized, that takes a lot of guts."

She wondered if it did, but nodded in a vague acceptance. She glanced aside finally, suddenly very conscious of his hard body so near. So familiar, so needed. "What about him?" she asked, nodding toward their captive.

"He's going to escape," Derek answered after a moment.

She looked up at him, puzzled. "Escape? But, why? I don't understand."

Derek seemed unusually indecisive for a moment, shaking his head slightly. "I'll explain later, all right? Why don't you wait here while I go set the stage?"

Still puzzled, Shannon sat down and leaned back against a tree when he left her, watching him move across the clearing and speak briefly to

Zach and Josh. After a few moments, Josh left them at the van and wandered over to his wife, who was still standing guard over their silent captive. He seemed to be teasing her, because both were smiling. Then he leaned over and kissed her cheek, and Shannon knew the driver didn't see or hear Josh whisper something to Raven; her face never changed expression.

Josh wandered back to the van, and the three men became engrossed in the task of defanging Cyrano. After a few minutes, Raven said something to the captive and then crossed the clearing to Shannon. "Hi."

"Is this where he escapes?" Shannon murmured, biting back a sudden and unexpected giggle.

Raven looked solemn. "I expect so. He's been trying very surreptitiously to work his arms down over his hips. If he managed that, and gets his hands in front of him, at least he can thumb a ride out of here. Minus Cyrano, of course."

Shannon resisted the urge to look over toward the man. "Um . . . why is he going to escape? Doesn't that give him the chance to call Moreton and spill the beans?"

Shrugging, Raven said, "It's Derek's plan, that's all I know. But I have a sneaking suspicion that Derek expects the guy to do something else once he gets away."

"For instance?"

"You'll have to ask Derek. I told you about his tactical genius, remember? Ten to one he's got this whole damned thing figured out point by point, by the numbers. Whether or not he'll tell *us*, however, is another matter. Plays his cards very close to his chest, Derek does."

Josh appeared at his wife's side and draped an arm across her shoulders. "You can get rid of the gat, Bonnie. The pigeon has flown the coop."

She gave him a pained look. "That's terrible."

"What? That he's gone?"

"No. Your gangsterish language."

"Just adding a little color to an otherwise dull afternoon," he defended himself stoutly.

Raven looked down at Shannon. "When he's like this, I can't do a thing with him."

Shannon was laughing in spite of everything.

Zach had been right on target when he estimated the time it would require to defang Cyrano. In just under two hours, the crate had been nailed shut again and the interior of the Civatech van restored to order.

After saying to Josh, "Stay out of trouble till I get back in Richmond, all right?" Zach climbed into the van and drove it back out onto the highway, heading for Norfolk.

"I hate to raise a tricky question," Josh said to Derek as they moved toward the helicopter, "but how do you know our escaped driver won't instantly call Moreton?"

Derek gave him a bland look. "Terrible about the phone lines, isn't it? Delicate things, susceptible to all kinds of tampering and damage."

"Talk about clout," Josh said a little blankly.

"Yes, but what about radio?" Raven asked interestedly. "Ship to shore? Or shore to ship?"

Derek helped Shannon into the helicopter and then paused to light a cigarette. "I don't think," he murmured, "they'll be able to fix their radio equipment until after they sail. The captain won't like to sail without it, but they have the spare parts aboard, and he has to keep to his schedule. Civatech's a little rabid about that."

There were no more questions until the helicopter was aloft, and then it was Shannon who leaned toward Derek and tried to make herself heard over the roar of the rotors.

"A fast car—"

Derek shook his head, and Shannon wasn't sure of what he said in response. She thought he said, "He won't go to Moreton," but there was so much noise . . . In any case, Derek seemed positive it wouldn't happen.

The two couples split up at the small airport where the helicopter had been rented, with Raven and Josh heading for their hotel and Derek and Shannon going back to the house. Derek circled the block once, studying the house as they passed, and must have been reassured enough to pull the car into the garage with no further checks.

It was early evening by then, and a somewhat strained silence fell between them as they shared the duties of preparing dinner. Shannon knew it was largely her fault: she was tense, a little nervous. For the first time, she felt as if it were nearly over. She was staring her future in the eye and didn't know what it held for her.

She needed Derek, and it frightened her. She'd never needed anyone before. Was she growing dependent, too dependent? Was that why she didn't know how she really felt about him, because of that dependency? She listened to her instincts, and they told her nothing.

Nothing at all.

· · ·

Derek had pushed as hard as he dared. He watched her that evening, and it hurt him to see her anxiety. He wanted to hold her, reassure her, love her. But Shannon had closed up, like a flower, and he couldn't force her to open without risking untold damage.

This was something she had to deal with herself, accept or not accept. He couldn't prove his love, any more than she could create it inside herself if it didn't already exist. He had done everything he could think of to banish that cracked mirror of hers: the rest was up to her.

When she slipped away at last to take a shower and get ready for bed, he wasn't surprised that she didn't return. She would be in her own room, her own bed, closing him out. He accepted that, even though it hurt, because he knew she was hurting too.

He got ready for bed himself, and before midnight darkness and silence had seeped into the house. Derek lay awake, wondering what the morning would bring, some instinct telling him that she would come to him.

And when she did come, in silence and need, he welcomed her with pleasure.

And pain.

Nine

There wasn't much, after all, that she had to take with her. Not much that was hers. She took only what she wore, slacks and a sweater, running shoes. In the dark silence, she dressed, grateful for the exhaustion that kept Derek sleeping soundly. In some distant part of her she was surprised that her movements didn't disturb him, as alert and wary as he was, but she knew he had gotten little rest these last days.

She didn't pause to look down at him, afraid that if she did, she'd never be able to leave. It was best, she told herself firmly, that she just leave. Leave right now, before he came to realize his feelings for her were based on the situation, the circumstances. Leave now, before he could begin to feel even more responsible for her.

She slipped out of the house in silence, brushing angrily at hot tears on her cheeks. She walked steadily, instinctively clinging to shadows and gazing around warily. She had no money, but soon found an all-night convenience store where a somewhat tough-looking woman allowed her to use the phone. After that, there was nothing to do but wait.

Shannon tried not to think. She tried not to feel. It was inevitable, of course, that she do both. During a single hectic, impossibly condensed week of her life, so much had happened that she knew nothing would ever be the same again. She looked at the world in a totally different way now, aware of dangers and deceptions.

And she looked at herself differently, understanding at last that everyone bore scars, just as Derek had said, and that hers were no worse than anyone else's. She felt ashamed that her own insecurities had occupied her mind so totally, when so many vital and dangerous decisions and choices were being made by strong and courageous people.

People like Derek, and Alexi, and Gina. People like Raven and Josh Long, and Zach Steele.

Especially people like Derek. She wished then that she could steal a few hours from time and just talk to him. Learn him. She wanted to know why he remained in his business despite the drawbacks and dangers, wanted to know about those choices he must have made over the years. She wanted to know what kept him going when there must have been times when he didn't want to go on, times when it would have been easier to just walk away.

Times when it would have been easier *not* to be strong.

And she wanted to thank him. Thank him, one human being to another, for being the man he was.

For teaching her so much about herself and others. Thank him for being a care-giver, for being patient and strong and the single constant in the turmoil of the last days.

It would have been so easy to go back to him right now. To crawl into bed beside him and just hold on to the warmth and strength he radiated. It would be so easy to let herself believe he loved her. To lose herself in that love until it wouldn't matter whether or not it was real.

Her instincts were silent.

Shannon drew a deep breath and leaned against the cold bricks behind her, staring blindly at the brightly lit parking lot, which was empty of cars. No. This once, just this once, she was going to be strong enough to take control of her life. She was walking away from Derek, steadily, not running in panic but walking, because it was the right thing for her to do. It was the only thing she could do in her uncertainty. Because she had to find the strength and courage to go on within herself, and not look helplessly to him for it.

That was it, really. She had never in her life depended on anyone else, and her dependence on Derek was unnerving. And that's all it was, of course, all she felt about him. It had to be that, because it made sense. Like a patient who fell in love with the doctor who saved her life, she had . . . she thought she had . . . but it wasn't *real*.

It couldn't be real.

She watched a dark car roll into the parking lot, and pushed herself away from the wall as it stopped a few feet away. The driver's door opened and he got out quickly, turning a tense and worried face to her.

"Shannon—"

"Hello, William."

Derek knew, the moment he came to full awareness, what had roused him from a sound sleep.
The room was utterly silent, dark and peaceful.
And the place beside him in bed was empty. He was
alone, and all his screaming senses told him that
she was not with him, that the house was empty
and had been for some time. Shannon was gone.

No one had taken her away from him, he knew
that. She had left on her own.

He was out of bed and dressing even before the
thought registered fully, his mouth dry and his
heart pounding heavily. It took precious moments
for him to dress and get what he needed from
where it lay high on a closet shelf, untouched for
so long, for what he had thought would be forever. It seemed like an eternity before he could go
after her. He was swearing inwardly, a toneless
and desperate litany, knowing that he had made
a terrible, deadly mistake in not telling her all he
knew and suspected.

She was out there, unaware that her trust was
a fatal weapon in cruel hands, innocently assuming that her own knowledge was correct. He had
wanted to shield her if possible, break the truth
to her gently, and only if necessary.

It was too late for that now. God help him, it
might be too late for Shannon.

His one mistake could get her killed.

Once outside the building, he hesitated and
then trusted his instincts, automatically turning
in a direction where there were lights in the dis-

tance, where he knew she would find businesses still open, people. She had no money, and she'd have to use a phone, he knew.

He walked as swiftly as he dared, his gaze scanning the dark streets and shadows carefully, his moccasins silent. He could hear his heart thudding, feel the hoarse rasp of breath in his throat. He had known fear before in his life, like any rational man, but the icy dread that gripped him now was unfamiliar and brutal. He wanted to cry out wildly to the night, shout some ringing command against time.

If she had only waited . . . Very soon it would be over, the events set in motion making her safe for good. But it was now, during these brief hours before morning, that she was the most vulnerable.

He should have told her.

He saw the convenience store and quickened his steps, fear clawing at his throat. Was he in time? He rounded the corner of the building just as a long black car rolled to a stop, and even as the other man stepped out and spoke, he heard his own voice emerge with utter calm.

"Hello, William."

Shannon felt her heart stop and then begin to pound heavily, and she looked to her left to see Derek standng a few feet away and gazing at William Franklin.

There was an instant of silence, almost as if everything had stopped, become frozen in an icy tableau of stillness, and then Franklin was smiling faintly at the other man. "Hello, Derek. Shannon called me."

"I know she did." Derek was looking at Franklin, not Shannon, and his voice was soft.

"I'll take her back with me," Franklin said, "so you can get on with whatever it is you have to do."

"No," Derek said.

The governor chuckled. "I don't blame you for wanting to keep her. But she's been through a lot, you know. It'll do her good to get some rest."

"Come with me, Shannon," Derek said, still looking at the governor.

Franklin sent her a reassuring smile. "You'll be better off with me, Shannon. Derek's sense of responsibility is working overtime, but you don't want to get in his way anymore."

"Bastard," Derek said tonelessly.

She looked from one to the other, bewildered, a chill of fear trickling down her spine. There was something wrong here, something terribly wrong. The two men were suddenly strangers, looking at each other with hard faces and cold, deadly eyes. And she was somehow in the middle, squarely between them, in a tug-of-war that was more than a game.

"I don't understand," she whispered.

"Come with me, Shannon," Franklin said, smiling at her with newly bright, warm eyes. "I've always taken care of you, haven't I? You know I'd never hurt you—I owe you my life. Come with me." He held out a hand to her.

"Shannon." Derek's voice was quiet, expressionless. "Trust me. Please trust me. Come to me."

On some detached level of herself, Shannon realized that she stood physically between them, and that neither could move, neither could get a clear—shot at the other. Shot? Why was she thinking that? *Why?* "I was leaving," she said.

"I know." Derek was still looking at Franklin, offering her nothing of reassurance in a glance or smile. "We'll talk about that. But come to me now."

The silence then was eternal, a screaming silence she didn't understand. But in that moment, the only certainty she felt was her certainty in Derek. It was a crystal-clear realization, stripped bare in a moment of stark need, and there was nothing muffled or distant about her feelings then, nothing unsure. For the first time since she had met Derek, she knew exactly what she was feeling, and knew why.

Without looking back, she turned away from Franklin and walked straight and steady into Derek's arms. She felt him shudder as he gathered her close, felt his chest rise and fall with harsh breaths, and then the strength and warmth of him surrounded her like a blanket of peace.

Derek had half turned as she reached him so that she was partially protected by him, by his powerful body, and she could see Franklin clearly as the governor stood stiffly, staring at them with a bitter look on his face. He took an abrupt step toward them, beginning to reach inside his coat, then halted as Derek freed one hand to pull a businesslike automatic from the small of his back and level it in a smooth, practiced movement.

Franklin didn't move. The utter shock on his face would have been amusing if the circumstances had been different. "I thought—but—you never use guns."

"I never have." Derek's voice was still quiet. "This time, there wasn't a choice."

Franklin nodded. "Because of her."

"She was almost killed, William. Do you really believe there's anything I wouldn't do to keep you from finishing the job?" There was nothing particularly cold or menacing about Derek's voice. It wasn't a loud voice, or a hard voice, or even a sharp voice. It was a gentle voice. But Shannon, held securely in the strong curve of his arm, shivered. And she saw Franklin's face go deathly pale.

"How long have you known?" the governor asked woodenly.

"Almost from the beginning. You gave Shannon someone to run to, William, and that wasn't like you. It didn't make sense to me that you suspected trouble at Civatech and yet didn't do anything about it. Not when you obviously cared so much about Shannon. I would have thought you'd get her into the governor's mansion instantly and then blow the whistle the moment you realized something was going on. But you didn't. It bothered me. And it bothered me to remember that blackmail threat against you years ago. A man can only be blackmailed when he's done something wrong. I knew of at least one very bad mistake you'd made in your career, a greedy mistake. It was entirely possible you'd gotten greedy again. And then, when your paid assassins found the loft so quickly, I knew it had to be you. No one else who was involved had the clout to find deeds with my name on it that fast."

"I never wanted her to be hurt," the governor said, almost pleading. "That's why I sent her to you. Moreton panicked and set that bomb in her apartment, it wasn't me. I made sure she knew to go to you. I knew you'd look out for her. But it was supposed to be over before you could act. I never counted on that shipping delay giving you time to get your hands on Cyrano. After that . . . I never had a choice, don't you see? I never had a choice. You had to be stopped."

"I could forgive you that, William," Derek said. "Going after me was the only practical thing to do—I was a threat. It's Shannon I can't forgive you for. Blowing up her home and nearly killing her. Having her hunted like an animal. There was no need for that, and you know it."

"It was Moreton who panicked and had the apartment—"

"You're responsible. Ultimately, you're responsible."

Franklin straightened shoulders that had slumped. "I see." He drew a deep, unsteady breath, and asked, "What are you going to do about it?"

"Your little toy's been disarmed. I let your driver go deliberately, William; I recognized him, and I knew he'd tell you Cyrano had been taken. I made sure you couldn't get in touch with Moreton. I knew it was the only way to draw you out. I thought you'd go for me. I didn't—I didn't expect Shannon to call you." He sighed roughly. "Anyway, it worked. We stopped the truck long enough to disarm the device and wipe the programming. And it was delivered, on time, in Norfolk. Moreton thinks he's delivering the real thing to Yaltan in person."

There was a sharp intake of breath from Franklin. "He'll be killed."

"Yes." Derek's voice was flat. "But before he's killed, he'll no doubt talk. Yaltan won't be happy with you, william. You'd better find a deep hole."

"I'm the governor," Franklin said, a last attempt at dignity and forcefulness.

"You're nothing." Derek sounded weary. "Leave office, resign in the morning. If you don't, I'll break the whole thing open before Yaltan gets the chance to."

There was an instant's silence, and then Franklin said constrictedly, "You're letting me go?"

"For her sake." His arm tightened around Shannon, and the gun never wavered. "Yaltan might get to you. He might not. But look over your shoulder for the rest of your life, William. One day, I'll be there."

"I sent her to you," Franklin said dully.

"Yes. That's the only reason you're still alive. Now get out of my sight."

With the jerky motion of a puppet with half its strings cut, Franklin turned and got into his car. A moment later, the dark car was rolling quietly out of the parking lot, and soon disappeared in the shadowy streets.

"Derek—"

"Shhh." The gun fell to his side as Derek turned her, keeping his arm around her and guiding her back the way they'd come. "We'll talk at the house, honey."

The tone of his voice, deadened and hollow, frightened her. She walked beside him in silence, grappling with the knowledge that it had been William all along, William who had intended to see her dead. That fact didn't feel quite real to her, and yet she believed it.

And she knew there was something else that had happened, something so vitally important that the knowledge of William's perfidy had been blunted in its impact on her. She had . . . what had she done?

She had chosen. With no idea of what was going on between the two men, she had been asked to trust only one of them. And she had done just that. Partly instinctively, but also consciously, she had chosen only one.

She should have chosen William over Derek. In her mind, he had been no threat, had been the good friend, undemanding, trustworthy. She had known him longer, trusted him longer. He hadn't made her nervous or wary, hadn't mixed up her emotions. Like the father she just barely remembered, he had represented stability and comfort and wisdom. The known quantity.

And Derek . . . a man who might well have done terrible things in the name of a greater good. A man who was adept in darkness and shadows. A man with old, sapphire-flecked eyes, and a hard, handsome face that had doubtless broken hearts. A man with scars, like her own. She had known him a matter of days, had been bewildered and unnerved by him, had felt wariness and mistrust and wild passion because of him. He had stripped away her walls with deliberate thoroughness, leaving her achingly vulnerable. He had held up a mirror to her soul and shown her a reflection she'd never seen before and could hardly believe.

And she had chosen him.

"Trust your instincts. There are moments when you have to make choices, especially in this world. And it's in those moments when your instincts will tell you the truth. Just listen to them."

And her instincts had finally answered.

Not just trust. Not just need. Love.

Shannon realized with a start that they had reached the house, that they were inside. She watched Derek turn on lights in the living room, and she felt light-headed and dizzy.

He looked down at the gun in his hand, and his mouth twisted. Flicking on the safety catch, he dropped the automatic into a chair with a weary gesture. "It's almost dawn," he said.

Shannon couldn't take her eyes off him. "Yes."

He avoided her gaze, rubbing the back of his neck as if it were tense. "It'll be safe for you soon. The news will break in a few hours about William's resignation," he said flatly. "You'll be able to leave then."

"Will I?"

A muscle tightened in his jaw. "Yes."

"Do you want me to?"

Derek turned away and went over to the window, staring out at a graying darkness. "It doesn't matter what I want," he said in a low voice. "You were leaving me. I've pushed you too hard, and I'm not going to do that again."

After a moment, she said, "I think I said once that love was—an illusion."

His shoulders tensed. "Mirrors and lights. I remember," he said in a rough tone.

"I was wrong."

Derek was still for a long minute, and then turned slowly to face her. He was a little pale, his expression masklike in its immobility. "What're you saying?" His voice was uneven.

"I shouldn't have chosen you," she said wonderingly. "By all rights, I shouldn't have chosen you. It wasn't because of trust; I trusted both of you. And

I didn't realize he'd done those—terrible things, so that wasn't it. I chose you because . . . because . . ."

He crossed the space between them in three steps, his hands lifting to catch her shoulders. "Shannon . . ."

"Because I love you." It was said on a sigh, astonishment and delight glowing in her eyes.

Derek pulled her against him suddenly, holding her possessively. "I hope you're sure, sweetheart," he said unsteadily, "because I love you too much to ever let you go."

"I've never been more sure of anything in my life," she told him, and in the tender heat of his kiss, she finally found the truth.

It didn't matter which world was real.

He was.

THE EDITOR'S CORNER

June is certainly a month for gorgeous, passionate, independent, loving, tender, daring, remarkable heroines! With three of the six women of the month being redheads, you can be sure to expect fireworks! Magdelena is washed right into her lover's arms in the rapids; Lux falls into her lover's arms with a giant teddy bear; Meghan has risky plans for her man; Candace finally wants to give all; Lacey's free spirit needs taming; and Randy learns to surrender . . . All this and a whole lot more in our June LOVESWEPTs. Read on to learn about each book and the wonderful heroes who fall in love with these six fabulous heroines.

In **CONFLICT OF INTEREST** by Margie McDonnell, LOVESWEPT #258, Magdelena Dailey, our heroine with long, wild hair, is rescued from a Colorado river by Joshua Wade who steals a passionate kiss as his reward. Joshua is a sweet seducer, a man made for love. Magdelena needs quite a bit of convincing before she changes her plans and lets a man into her life again, and Joshua is up to the challenge. There's no resisting his strong arms and tender smile, and soon Magdelena is riding the rapids of love!

Lux Sherwood is a raven-haired beauty in **WARM FUZZIES**, LOVESWEPT #259, by one of our perennial favorites, Joan Elliott Pickart. All Lux needs is one of her very own creations—a giant teddy bear—to get Patrick "Acer" Mullaney's attention. Acer is a star quarterback with a serious injury that's keeping him out of the game—the game of football, that is. He's definitely strong enough to participate in the game of love, and here's just a taste of what Acer has to say to Lux:

> "My needs run in a different direction. I need to kiss you, hold you, touch you. I need to make love to you until I'm too exhausted to move. I don't want to be just your friend, Lux. I won't be."

(continued)

What's a woman to say to such a declaration? Lux finds the right words, and the right actions in **WARM FUZZIES!**

We're so pleased to bring you our next LOVESWEPT for the month, **DIVINE DESIGN,** #260, by first novelist Mary Kay McComas. With a redheaded heroine like Meghan Shay and her daring scheme, we're certain that Mary Kay McComas is headed for LOVESWEPT success! Her hero in **DIVINE DESIGN** isn't bad either! Who can resist a long, tall Texan whose eyes gleam with intelligence *and* naked desire. Michael Ramsey has all the qualifications that Meghan is looking for—in fact he's too perfect, too good looking, too kind, too wonderful—and she can't help but fall in love, and that's not part of Meghan's plans. Ah, the best laid plans . . .

Barbara Boswell delivers another moving love story with **BABY, BABY,** LOVESWEPT #261. By popular demand, Barbara brings you Candace "Barracuda" Flynn's love story. And what a love story it is! Candace wants a second chance with Nick Torcia, but Nick is wary—as well he should be. Candace burned him once, and he isn't coming back for more. But something has changed. Precious new babies have brought them both an understanding of love. Still, Nick needs to lay the past to rest. Here's a sample of the intensity of their encounter:

"Why did you lead me on, Candy?" Nick demanded, his onyx eyes burning into hers.

"Not for revenge," she whispered.

"Then why, Candy?"

Her heart seemed to stop beating. He was so close to her, close enough for her to feel the heat emanating from his hard, masculine frame.

"Nick." His name escaped from her throat in a husky whisper, and she tried to move closer. Desire, sharp as a stiletto, sliced through her. She wanted to lose herself in his arms, to feel his hot, hard mouth take hers. She gazed at him with undisguised yearning.

But Nick wouldn't let her close the gap between them. He held her wrists, controlling her movements and keeping her anchored in place. "Tell me, Candy."

Tyler Winter is the man who tames Lacey Lee Wilcox's free spirit in **FOR THE LOVE OF LACEY,** LOVESWEPT #262, by Sandra Chastain. Tyler is a renaissance man—an artist, businessman, and an absolutely irresistible hunk! Is

(continued)

he a flirt or really a man Lacey can trust her heart to? Tyler showers her with kisses, gives her wildflowers, and takes her on picnics, but still Lacey is afraid of losing her heart. With just a little more convincing our heroine loses her fears and listens to her heart:

"Tyler, turn me loose," Lacey ordered.

"Nope," he said, moving his mouth toward hers.

Not again, she begged silently. Too late. She was being kissed, thoroughly kissed, and there was no way to stop him. Tyler finally drew back and grinned down at her with undisguised joy.

"Tyler," she protested, "you don't know what you're doing."

"You're right, and it's been a long time since ignorance felt so good. Kiss me, Lacey."

In **HAWK O'TOOLE'S HOSTAGE** by Sandra Brown, LOVESWEPT #263, Randy Price can't believe what's happening to her. It's 1987, yet she's just been abducted by a masked man on a horse! No, this is not part of the old west show she was watching with her son. Who is this masked man? And why does he want Randy? Hawk O'Toole is an Indian Chief with very good and honorable reasons for kidnapping Randy Price, but he doesn't plan on the intense attraction he feels toward her. She's his hostage, but fate turns the tables, and he becomes her slave. Love has a way of quieting the fiercest battles as Randy and Hawk find out.

Happy Reading! Remember to look for The Hometown Hunk Contest next month—it's your big chance to find the perfect LOVESWEPT hero!

Sincerely,

Kate Hartson

Kate Hartson
    Editor

LOVESWEPT
Bantam Books.
666 Fifth Avenue
New York, NY 10103

ENTER
THE DELANEYS, THE UNTAMED YEARS
MISSISSIPPI QUEEN' RIVERBOAT CRUISE
SWEEPSTAKES
W I N
7 NIGHTS ABOARD THE LUXURIOUS
MISSISSIPPI QUEEN STEAMBOAT
**including double occupancy accommodations,
meals and fabulous entertainment for two**

She's elegant. Regal. Alive with music and moonlight. You'll find
a Jacuzzi, gym, sauna, movie theatre, gift shop, library, beauty
salon and multi-tiered sun deck aboard…plus a splendid dining
room and lounges, beveled mirrors, polished brass, a Grand
Saloon where big band sounds soothe your soul and set your feet
to dancing! For further information and/or reservations on the
Mississippi Queen and Delta Queen' Steamboats
CALL 1-800-458-6789!

Sweepstakes travel arrangements by
RELIABLE TRAVEL INTERNATIONAL, INC.

Whether you're travelling for business, romance or adventure,
you're a winner with Reliable Travel International!
CALL TOLL FREE FOR INFORMATION AND RESERVATIONS
1-800-645-6504 Ext. 413

**MISSISSIPPI QUEEN RIVERBOAT CRUISE SWEEPSTAKES
RULES AND ENTRY FORMS ALSO APPEAR IN THE
FOLLOWING BANTAM LOVESWEPT NOVELS:**

THE GRAND FINALE	**MAN FROM HALF MOON BAY**
HOLD ON TIGHT	**OUTLAW DEREK**
***CONFLICT OF INTEREST**	***DIVINE DESIGN**
***WARM FUZZIES**	***BABY, BABY**
***FOR LOVE OF LACEY**	***HAWK O'TOOLE'S HOSTAGE**

and in

**THE DELANEYS, THE UNTAMED YEARS:
COPPER FIRE; WILD SILVER; GOLDEN FLAMES**

*On sale week of May 2, 1988   SW'10

OFFICIAL DELANEYS, THE UNTAMED YEARS
MISSISSIPPI QUEEN' RIVERBOAT CRUISE
SWEEPSTAKES RULES

1. NO PURCHASE NECESSARY. Enter by completing the Official Entry Form below (or print your name, address, date of birth and telephone number on a plain 3"x 5" card) and send to:

> Bantam Books
> Delaneys, THE UNTAMED YEARS Sweepstakes
> Dept. HBG
> 666 Fifth Avenue
> New York, NY 10103

2. One Grand Prize will be awarded. There will be no prize substitutions or cash equivalents permitted. Grand Prize is a 7-night riverboat cruise for two on the luxury steamboat, The Mississippi Queen. Double occupancy accommodations, meals and on-board entertainment included. Round trip airfare provided by Reliable Travel International, Inc. (Estimated retail value $5,500.00. Exact value depends on actual point of departure.)

3. All entries must be postmarked and received by Bantam Books no later than August 1, 1988. The winner, chosen by random drawing, will be announced and notified by November 30, 1988. Trip must be completed by December 31, 1989, and is subject to space availability determined by Delta Queen Steamboat Company, and airline space availability determined by Reliable Travel International. If the Grand Prize winner is under 21 years of age on August 1, 1988, he/she must be accompanied by a parent or guardian. Taxes on the prize are the sole responsibility of the winner. Odds of winning depend on the number of completed entries received. Enter as often as you wish, but each entry must be mailed separately. Bantam Books is not responsible for lost, misdirected or incomplete entries.

4. The sweepstakes is open to residents of the U.S. and Canada, except the Province of Quebec, and is void where prohibited by law. If the winner is a Canadian he/she will be required to correctly answer a skill question in order to receive the prize. All federal, state and local regulations apply. Employees of Reliable Travel International, The Delta Queen Steamboat Co., and Bantam, Doubleday, Dell Publishing Group, Inc., their subsidiary and affiliates, and their immediate families are ineligible to enter.

5. The winner may be required to submit an Affidavit of Eligibility and Promotional Release supplied by Bantam Books. The winner's name and likeness may be used for publicity purposes without additional compensation.

6. For an extra copy of the Official Rules and Entry Form, send a self-addressed stamped envelope (Washington and Vermont Residents need not affix postage) by June 15, 1988 to:

> Bantam Books
> Delaneys, THE UNTAMED YEARS Sweepstakes
> Dept. HBG
> 666 Fifth Avenue
> New York, NY 10103

- -

OFFICIAL ENTRY FORM
DELANEYS, THE UNTAMED YEARS
MISSISSIPPI QUEEN' RIVERBOAT CRUISE SWEEPSTAKES

Name _____

Address _____

City _____ State _____ Zip Code _____

SW 10

THE DELANEY DYNASTY

Men and women whose loves and passions are so glorious it takes many great romance novels by three bestselling authors to tell their tempestuous stories.

THE SHAMROCK TRINITY

- ☐ 21786 RAFE, THE MAVERICK
  by Kay Hooper $2.75
- ☐ 21787 YORK, THE RENEGADE
  by Iris Johansen $2.75
- ☐ 21788 BURKE, THE KINGPIN
  by Fayrene Preston $2.75

THE DELANEYS OF KILLAROO

- ☐ 21872 ADELAIDE, THE ENCHANTRESS
  by Kay Hooper $2.75
- ☐ 21873 MATILDA, THE ADVENTURESS
  by Iris Johansen $2.75
- ☐ 21874 SYDNEY, THE TEMPTRESS
  by Fayrene Preston $2.75

- ☐ 26991 THIS FIERCE SPLENDOR
  by Iris Johansen $3.95

THE DELANEYS: *The Untamed Years*

- ☐ 21897 GOLDEN FLAMES *by Kay Hooper* $3.50
- ☐ 21898 WILD SILVER *by Iris Johansen* $3.50
- ☐ 21999 COPPER FIRE *by Fayrene Preston* $3.50

Buy these books at your local bookstore or use the handy coupon below.

- -

Bantam Books, Dept. SW9, 414 East Golf Road, Des Plaines, IL 60016

Please send me the books I have checked above. I am enclosing $_____ (please add $2.00 to cover postage and handling). Send check or money order—no cash or C.O.D.s please.

Mr/Ms _____

Address _____

City/State _____ Zip _____

SW9—5/88

Please allow four to six weeks for delivery. This offer expires 11/88. Prices and availability subject to change without notice.